A Quentin Forberg

MW00782549

i want to break

Cover Art by Elena Gatti

A Tree District Books Publication

Tree District Books, LLC is the publisher. It holds the license with respect to this work and any derivatives thereof on a worldwide basis. Please visit www.treedistrictbooks.com for more information or to contact the publisher.

ISBN: 978-1-951072-07-0

Chapter 1 - Talk to Me

I knew I would meet you. It took all summer.

Can you hear me?

Listen. I really don't want to die. Please talk to me. I'll say what you want me to say. Okay?

Okay. Here I go. Oh, I don't know...

I've been thinking about what's wrong with me. I couldn't find much of an answer. I know I'm bad. I know most people are bad. And since everyone's bad, then we're all the same. But I know I'm a special kind of bad. I can feel it. I'm scared and emotional. I twitch. My muscles are always bouncing around in my body. I'm addicted. I float around. And it's okay. I was irrational. I wasn't thinking straight. I hadn't met you. Now, I'm rational. I see why I'm so bad and why everyone else is so bad. It's when you don't have answers. The thing I've realized is that when you don't have an answer, you just sink. So, you find something and you cling to it. That's why I love you so much. I feel right. I feel good. I know what is happening and I know I shouldn't be afraid-

I keep rambling... I'm sorry. I'll say everything.

I guess I'll start from the beginning. That brings me to May. And my house and booze and acid. It's almost August now. And we're still at my house and I'm drunk and tripping. Some things won't change. It's okay.

The first time I ever took acid was back at school. I was in my tiny dorm room and now that I think of it, that was the best day of my life. I'm afraid it always will be. I'll never feel alive and smart and understanding like that again.

I'm sorry. I just want to explain everything at the beginning so you don't feel lost. And maybe you'll understand who I am. I'll try to be honest. Have you ever been honest? I don't know... I hope it's a good thing.

So here's the beginning. My mom and sister went out of town. They left for the whole summer. At the end of the school year, I started looking for jobs. There weren't any internships for me. After sophomore year, it's tough to find that kind of thing. Unless you're connected. But both of my parents are teachers. I'm an engineering student. Instead, I got a job with my buddies working for Mrs. O'Malley. It was fine. It was fun actually. We were left alone to do our work and the work was mostly easy. Manual labor like that isn't bad. Not many people would call landscaping manual labor, though. Mrs' O'Malley paid us in cash too, and she knew where it was going. But we did good work.

So my dad had to meet up with my mom and sister, leaving me all alone. Since no one else was around, I drove him to the airport. For some reason, I wanted to tell him about my acid trip. I don't know why. I just did. At first, I was nervous. Then, I told him. He looked at me and shook his head and didn't talk to me for the rest of the ride. He was pissed and just walked off to security after I pulled up to the curb. And he's deathly afraid of flying. It's his phobia. That's when I realized I did a good thing. And I thought to myself. Finally...

Chapter 2 - Lawmen

It's Friday. 7 P.M. The sun is just setting. I was lucky to drive west as there was a redness and then a purple in the sky. I'm back at O'Hare airport. I don't know why he's flying in. He's from Indiana and working downtown. But I'm happy he's coming to stay with me. I like him. He's a good person.

The rows of red lights blink in front of me as we all edge forwards through the tight cement walls.

The grooves in the cement make a rumbling noise under the car even though I'm going pretty slow. The windows are down and I'm listening to Tame Impala. Their really early stuff. It sounds perfect in the humid air with the slight breeze rustling my hair. Guy texts me. He just grabbed his suitcase off the carousel. I throw on my blinker and force myself past a minivan and put on my hazards. The metronome clicks. A woman in an orange vest watches me from along the curb. I text Guy to hurry up. They're watching. Timing us. They need to keep the line in motion. That's all I know.

He comes jogging over dragging a large black suitcase. Even from here, I can hear the plastic wheels tapping the grooves in the cement sidewalk. I love that sound. It's not nearly as invasive as the rumbling. But the rumbling catches your attention. And I'm always bored when I drive.

"Yo!" says Guy. He's opening the backdoor and throwing his suitcase along the seats.

"Hey, man-" I say.

"Tame Impala?"

"Yeah."

"Good shit... Seems like their new stuff-"

"It's okay."

"Nah. It's just bad."

"It's all right."

"Think about it for a second. Remember how it sounds. Doesn't that piss you off?"

"I guess. A little."

"Well, they changed. That's usually a good thing." He pauses for a second. "Forget that, man. I've gotta be more positive."

"Don't worry about it."

"I'm serious. This is gonna be a good summer."

"I agree. How was the flight?"

"No problem at all. You know, I like flying. It keeps things interesting."

"Where the hell were you anyways?"

"L.A." He puts his hands down on the dash. "I've got something to tell you."

"What?"

He pauses.

"I'm thinking of moving out there."

"What? Why?"

"I don't know. A few of my friends. My best friends are already out there. I think I want to go out there with them."

"Aren't you working downtown? And living with me?"

I edge through all the huddled cars and switch three lanes to the left. Lots of honks. Drivers lifting their necks up to get a better look. Turning their music down. That part never makes sense to me. I guess all the noise and commotion is stifling. Kinda messes your head up.

"No. I quit that." He was quiet for a while. "Not gonna lie, it was horrible. I had a horrible time downtown. And I have enough money saved up now until I find something out there. I realized I should just do it. There's not gonna be anything left, here. I've gotta be more positive."

"Well. You gotta do what you gotta do. L.A. could be fun…"

I tap on the steering wheel and make my way towards the Kennedy. The clicks of my turning signal. "Especially with your best friends."

"Yeah. Exactly. It's a big change. But fuck it. I'm tired of sitting around and waiting. And you know, change can be good"

"It can be."

"We're gonna have the whole summer, though." He starts laughing. "I don't even have a fucking job-"

We both lean back and let the cool wind blow our hair and wipe the sweat from our foreheads and necks. A family trait. I drive through the night as the rows of fluorescent spotlights flood the road with white light and soon the skyline appears far away, in the distant night. It is beautiful. Guy always points it out when he's in Chicago. Even though he worked there and it's no longer new and different. But now, we agree that there's something fake about it. Its beauty. Now he just laughs at it. People say it's a testament to humanity's greatness, but is it really? Yeah. I guess it is. I just don't know how so many people could actually work together to make all that shit. No, I do. It's money. That's why.

"We've gotta make a stop-" says Guy.

"Where at?" I ask.

"I think it's near your house. I still don't know all the neighborhoods. I just know it's on the Southside. It's definitely not like Indiana. We just have towns."

"What's the neighborhood?"

"Evergreen Park... I'm pretty sure that's what he said."

"Yeah. Yeah. That's right by my house. How the hell do you know someone from there?"

"I met him at school."

"Everyone knows someone from everywhere from school."

"What the hell." Guy is laughing. "What does that even mean?"

I blush a little.

"I don't know, man."

The house is nice for Evergreen Park. That neighborhood is shit. All the kids from there I know from high school are scumbags. Coke heads. I don't like coke heads. They always take themselves too seriously. Anybody who takes drugs regularly takes themselves too seriously. That's why I have a timeframe. I like to wait 3 months between doses. Otherwise it's too much. I'm hoping Guy isn't picking up coke like that. He still hasn't told me anything.

A man Guy's age runs out from the front door and hops in the backseat. I don't know his face but his cargo pockets are stuffed. His t-shirt is red and faded. But I couldn't see much of it. A dark backpack hangs down his butt. He tells me to take a ride around the block and to keep my head up.

I pull up to a stop sign on 90th street and take a right. The streetlights are shut off and the man in the back is shuffling through the backpack. His phone's flashlight is on and darting all over the ceiling. Lighting up the gray fuzz. The houses are back to normal. One story ranches with wide pale windows. I can hardly see them through the darkness but TVs are glaring through invisible walls. There is the sound of shuffling plastic. In the mirror, I see a gallon Ziploc bag full of something. All Guy says is nice as the man zips the backpack shut. Now, they are whispering.

A second stop sign. I slow down. There's a black car to my right. Hidden in the darkness. No street lights here, too. I see the metal stalks rising, barely opaque lines in the night. I turn my blinker on. The metronome clicks and Guy and the man are quiet.

A flood light ignites the intersection. It's coming from a little bulb hooked up to the other car. Right above the driver's side mirror. Fuck me. Undercover cops. I know there's something bad behind me in the back seat. Guy and the man are silent. Guy has his shoulders back against the seat and he's staring straight ahead.

My car is moving slowly. I drive through the invasive light and it gets in my eyes a bit. I'm squinting. But I keep driving slowly. I do not look up at the other car. Holy shit, that dude better have his backpack under his feet. He's gotta know. He fuckin' better. Guy shushes and I keep driving.

The floodlight is behind me now and I see the cop car moving forward. The red lights dim in my rear view. He goes through the intersection and soon, the floodlight clicks off. I see no black outline as the red rear lights click off. Just black. The car returns to its invisible nature, hunting in the night. I sigh shakily. The man sighs in the back then scoffs.

"They're always around." I say. My heart is pounding.

"Yeah, they are. Just shut up." says Guy while laughing.

The man in the back sighs one more time. "Those motherfuckers are always out and about. They don't have anything better to do. I don't get it, man... And Guy, why the fuck did you shush me? What the hell was that gonna do?"

"I don't know, man! I panicked. I don't know much about these Chicago cops."

"Well, if you're in a car, it doesn't matter if you're quiet..." says the man. He's laughing now.

"It really doesn't matter," I say.

I laugh quietly and I look at the man in the rear-view mirror. Maybe he'll like me. I should say a funny joke. But Guy laughs. Then we all laugh. Now it's silent.

I drop off the man and I drive us back to Western and down 95th street. The shops are all closed. Or abandoned. The old Borders on Claremont is completely empty inside, but the red letters still adorn the faded brick. The Joint is still open.

Guy and I stop in and sit at a booth in the back corner. A young girl from the neighborhood is our waitress. She's Irish. Dark eyes. Dark curly hair. Pale Skin. Freckles. Black Irish. I order the deluxe cheeseburger and a chocolate shake. Guy does the same. Without cheese. I like to dip my fries in mayo so I ask for an extra container.

"When was the last time you came here?" I ask.

11

"Man…" says Guy. "It's been years. We're never in town for Grandma's birthday. Or anyone's, for that matter."

"That's true. I hardly come here with anyone other than my Dad now. I don't know why."

"When did your parents leave?"

The waitress brings the food over. It smells delicious. I stop talking and wait for her to walk away. But she smiles over at Guy and he looks back at me.

"My dad's been there for a couple days. My mom and sister, almost a month."

"Damn. You know, I'm jealous. There's something over there. You can go to Cathedrals and shit. Can you do that here?"

"I think we have Cathedrals."

"Yeah these are our Cathedrals…" Guy laughs and bites into his burgers and juices squirt out and run down his fingers. "Not like there. Look at us. This is the culture we have. This is what we worship, man. But don't worry, it's sophisticated."

He points around the diner and we both peer around. The grease slicked floor, the obese couple in the booth across gorging themselves, the smell of oil. The paneling shriveling from the humidity, the cheap motel paintings, the chipped brown plastic beneath my legs. The dripping cheeseburger, the thick fries. The fake plants and fake mulch and fake dirt, the group of cops sitting in the back, voices booming.

"I can't eat now." I say after a while.

"I'm sorry. I don't mind this place. I really don't. I'm just being too honest… But imagine being in France now!" says Guy. "Or anywhere real. Like L.A."

His eyes are wild and excited. I am just flat.

"Believe me…" I look around the restaurant. I wish I was. "But we're gonna have fun, man. We're definitely gonna have a good time."

"Yeah. Forget I said anything, okay. That's what I was saying. I've gotta be more positive. Laugh about it. I'll show you what I got for us when we get home."

"Nice."

"You're into acid, right?"

"Hell yeah."

"Good."

We finish and pay and I drive us home.

Guy unpacks and gets ready for bed. I watch some TV like every night. I try to convince myself to read but I'm lazy. I have work tomorrow. I don't know why I think it's work to read now. I used to love it. I still do. But maybe I'm just a lazy bastard now. Maybe that's why I'm so bad. But I'm in bed now. My laptop is playing some TV show and I can feel the warmth from the machine on the bed and I stare at the ceiling in the darkness. My bedroom is too hot. The air is thick and the ceiling fan is ticking up there. Fucking metronome. I have to be up early. The fan's on in the window blaring a calming white noise. Click. Click. Click. Fuck it. I'll smoke. I need to sleep, though. Yeah, let's sleep. Okay.

Chapter 3 - First Day of Work

The sun is sharp. My blue blinds don't reach the edges of the windows. There is nowhere to hide. A pillow covers my face but the light finds a way in. My skin is damp. My hair is damp. The sheets are damp beneath my back. Pimples will grow on my shoulders and blister in the sun under my cotton shirt. It's okay. I don't really mind.

I rub the skin beneath my eyes, and I lift myself and walk to the shower. I've been trying this thing. Saw it on the internet. Probably a bunch of bullshit. I leave the water on cold and hop in. It scares your body at first then it feels good. So I finish and tie a towel around my waist and walk to my bedroom to put on shorts and a t-shirt and high socks. I make coffee and eat a banana. The coffee is hazelnut flavored and tastes good with the banana.

Guy's been here for a week. I haven't seen much of him. He's always on his computer. But that's fine.

The truck will be here soon. Mrs. O'Malley said we were going to a nice old lady's house. Maybe we will get lunch out of it. Usually, nice old ladies give us lunch or lemonade. I sit on the swing on my front porch and wait.

The truck is white and some parts are rusty. Cracks run around the wheels and hubcaps. There is a wheelbarrow flipped over in the back and Mrs. O'Malley honks again as she pulls up. My friend Luke is sitting in the front seat. His head is resting against the window and he is wearing a baseball hat. Shit, I should've grabbed one.

I hop up the back bumper and climb into the bed and sit along the metal box tethered to the cabin and lean against the back window. There are many trees on my block. The sun is filtered golden as it breaks through the oak and sometimes it glints in my eyes. The houses and trees and cars shrink in front of me and the wind blows my hair down on my face. I feel peaceful some mornings, when I'm distracted. I'm happy to be seeing my friends. I like working with them. The wind feels good and I bounce with every crack. My body rattles as we go over tracks and I swing with every turn. We are going to a house just past the bar street. By Saint John Fisher. I don't like that area.

The sun is beginning to feel hot as we pull up. I will sweat a lot today. I think Mrs. O'Malley is just dropping us off. It's me and Luke for now. John and Bob will be meeting us later. I grew up with these guys.

"Okay, guys. Ready?" says Mrs. O'Malley. She's always full of energy with wide eyes and a loud laugh. Very nice woman. I like her a lot.

First, she brings me to the back portion of the yard. She tells me to weed here, between the fuchsias and other bushes. There's creeping charlie and dandelions. Luke will be weeding the other side and we should meet in the middle. Josh and Bob will be here later to help you plant bushes. Then, you'll be done. She tells us to get our set ups and smiles and tells us she's going to another house.

I am on my knees. The dirt is cool in the shade and it's even a little soft. But my knees are getting dirty and small wood chips are poking into my skin. I use my trowel to stab the earth beneath the root and push hard with my palm into the wooden handle. I hear a small snap and I know the root is cut. Mrs' O'Malley always tells us to get to the roots. Or else there's no point. The dandelions are the best. There is one large root that you snap through pretty easily. Then the whole plant comes out in one pull. The creeping charlie is different. There are many different roots that you have to pull up individually and sometimes you miss them so the next time you're in the garden, they've grown right back. I don't think they ever go away. Maybe when they're dead in the winter.

The sun is hot and it's beating down on my back and Luke is doing the same as me on the other side. He is a good worker.

"It's gonna be a hot one." he says. His voice is soft and monotone. It's good while working.

"Yeah… I'm not ready for it, man. You got water?" I say.

"Yeah. You?"

"Yeah. Thank god."

"You hungover?"

"Not today."

"Yeah. Me neither."

"What are you doin' tonight?"

My shoulders are getting tired from the digging and I'm sweating. The sun hurts my neck, too. I think it's starting to burn.

"No idea…"

"I was gonna take acid with my cousin. I'm thinking I'm gonna throw a party, too."

"Yeah? On acid?"

"Yeah. Fuck it. Know what I mean? What's the worst thing that could happen?"

"Have a good time, that's what. My brother does that all the time at school."

"That's what I'm saying. We were thinking of taking it early in the afternoon… We're done soon right?"

"Yeah. I'm betting around noon or one."

"Hell yeah."

I am crouched now, reaching behind one of the bushes to retrieve some of the creeping charlie. I'm using the side of my trowel to scrape the roots from the dirt but I'm not getting all of it. That's okay. No one will notice. But sometimes small branches from the bushes scratch my arms. I have all these little scabs now running up and down my forearms. Our voices are nearing each other. We're close to being done. We have another plot of dirt to weed after. Then, Josh and Bob will be here.

"I heard they got in some shit last night-" says Luke.

"They always are-" I say.

"*We* always are."

"How many times have I found your ass sleeping in the grass?"

"Too many times- What about you though?"

We laugh and empty our buckets of weeds and dirt and insects into the trash cans at the side of the garage and sit on the patio in wicker chairs. I look to the sky. There are traces of clouds, wisps dangling above us and the sun evaporates them. It is slowly climbing across the sky and I am going to be happy to see it straight above me, burning the crown of my head.

Luke is sipping his water looking at his phone. I check mine. Guy texted me. He's not gonna be home today. He has to fly back to L.A. Already? I text him. Now I wait. My water is getting warm, even in the shade and my arms are slick with sweat, grains of dirt, and blood. We begin weeding over by the garage, working meticulously. It is not hard work.

A car honks and Michael and Bob march through the back gate. They are both smiling and holding shovels on their shoulders.

"Yo!" says Michael. He shakes my hand and then Luke's. Bob is silent but he still shakes our hands. They are sweaty and muddy too. But smiling. We are all smiling.

"Let's plant these mofuckin' bushes and get outta here!" says Michael. He is inspecting the back garden looking for open plots of land.

"How many are there?" I ask.

"I think just 3," says Michael. "They're in the trunk."

"Imma go get em'," says Luke.

Michael tosses the shovels down and follows Luke back through the gate. I hear the trunk close and they walk back in holding three more fuchsias.

"I guess that makes it easy then". I say. "Right by the other ones."

"Makes sense, right?" says Michael.

"Why does she want more fuschias?" I say.

"I don't care. If she's gonna pay us, I don't care…" says Luke.

"But who needs more fuchsias? What do fuchsias do?"

"They sit there and look good I guess…" says Luke.

"Just like you, Luke," says Michael. "Do we really need any more Lukes?"

I pause and think.

"Yeah, we do," says Luke while laughing.

"I don't know, man." I say.

"You're gonna do me like that?" says Luke.

"Nah… It's just who the fuck needs more fushias."

We take our shovels and dig three holes. Maybe 6 inches deep. A little bit deeper. We push the fuchsia roots and we hold up the plants as another fills the whole back up. We repeat this three times.

"We getting paid today?" says Luke.

"No idea," I say.

"Ehh," says Luke.

I turn to Michael and Bob. "Can I get a ride home?"

"Yeah, man. Let's go."

Chapter 4 - Acid

I told them 9 o'clock for the party. I told them to invite people too. It doesn't matter how many people show up. Who cares?

Guy texts me. He already has an interview out in L.A. I don't know who with. I don't think he really cares. The last few days he's been applying to a shit ton of places. He always had this real anxious look on his face. Like he was about to drown. I guess if you're living at your dumbass cousin's house, you've got a reason to be anxious. He just wants to get out there and away from here.

It's not so bad here. I'm still happy for him. I'm going to take the acid without him.

I shower and put on clean clothes. I drink water and prepare the basement. My lightshow. My lasers. Spread them out onto the white brick wall and my headphones sit on the arm rest. I figured I'd be coming down by the time my friends were coming over. Time to drink. Not right now. I am watching TV in the living room for the beginning. I put one tab on my tongue and wait a bit and swallow. Small dose. I wasn't going for the big thing today. I didn't want to be alone for that. It terrifies me. I don't want to exist, but I can't let myself not exist. I need someone to hold me and tell me everything's okay when I come back from that. I will be like a little baby. Afraid of my own shadow. Reborn. I want to dip my toes back in now. Remember what it's like. It's been a while.

I let my dog out the back door and soon my legs feel wobbly. There is a feeling bubbling in my stomach. A lightness. A happiness. It travels up to my eyeballs and the backs of my cornea, feeling, bulging. In a good way. A happy way. I follow him down the back steps and watch as he sprints in roundabout circles between the ferns and rose bushes, following the same bubbling path. There is a look in his eyes. A look of understanding. This is what he does, and what he is supposed to do. He will forever. He is the most beautiful dog in the world. So I stop him and hug him and he talks to me in my mind and I understand how beautiful everything is. Thanks, Max.

I sit down on the couch and lean back. The corners of the living room are growing and retracting, and the walls are breathing. My body feels good now. It is tingling everywhere. I missed that. I can't stop smiling. The yellow paint on the walls is starting to glow. The sunshine from outside is getting brighter too. The walls are wavy and now the windows and everything is blended together in this fluid motion. Everything is moving together.

I walk to the basement. It is dark down there. There is a small button on the lower rim of the lightshow and when I click it, rippling colors wash across the white wall. The blue reminds me of the ocean. And it is peaceful. Sometimes the ocean can be terrifying but sometimes it can be peaceful. It can drag out by your toes and dangle you and pull you into its dark depths or lap at your ankles while your toes rest in soft sand. I click again. The yellow is boring to me. I do not like it. I click twice and the machine has a mind of its own so I sit in my chair and lean back because my body is both heavy and light. But when the deep purple comes sweeping in after the green I feel a growing bubble in my body and then the blue comes and it is perfect and beautiful and that feeling settles around all of my skin. Now I am weightless. My body has ceased to be flesh.

And the music is so good. Oh my god. I am so happy. Oh my god. The music is so good.

I want the purple to come back. Every time I see it I get closer to that feeling. It builds me up and up and then I am laid back down like a gentle wind blowing a young leaf. That is how my body feels in the small armchair. Floating in the breeze. Come back purple. Yes.

I am stuck here. The colors are staying the same and I'm feeling the same. I want more. I always want more. What is going to get me more? I do not want to smoke weed. Time? But I cannot be patient. It feels so good.

So I lay there with my headphones on and the colors change shapes and each color is a different sound and I see something new with every feeling and sound and my body feels so good. And I am okay. I am okay with being here.

I am bored now. I am not tripping that hard. I haven't understood, I've only observed. None of my thoughts are really connecting. That's when acid gets good. When everything starts to make sense and you feel great. It's just not happening right now. It pisses me off. I am kind of sad about that but it's okay. I don't want to be angry. Sad is okay. I won't do anything bad to myself.

I walk up the stairs and lay down in my bed. It is still damp from this morning, and the humidity hangs close to my skin. Breathing is not easy. The lights are off but a different light floats through the windows. It is white and faint. Everything else is hidden. Nothing but shadows. I turn on my laptop. It is going to be dark outside soon. Where are my friends?

I am going to read about when people go all the way. It will not happen to me now. That is okay. I will need someone to cradle my head, then. I want to go all the way so bad but I'm scared.

So, it is sudden. I will see myself drift away and I will forget who I am and what everything is. I'll look at my own hands and see aliens. I'll talk to speckles of matter. I'll look down and see blackness. Okay. Okay. Will it be scary? I hope not. God, why am I doing this? Why am I thinking this? I shouldn't think this. I'm going to make myself crazy. I'm gonna be crazy. The thought's looping. Oh fuck. My parents. Fuck. My parents would be so mad. My dad wouldn't be able to look at me. Fuck. It's too dark in here. There are dark shapes following me even when I close my eyes and hide. Oh fuck. Holy fuck. I can't think about this. My body is tingling. Not good. It is panicking. My eyes are darting around the room and my eyes are making shapes. Who is that? Are my parents here? Did they ever leave? Am I alone?

I am traveling down a giant waterslide and the water is pitch black and the surface is invisible and there is no sky or sun. There is no me. I am falling and swirling and there is nothing for me to hold onto and I am falling and I am swirling.

"Yo!"

My head snaps up. There is a figure at the door.

"Yo! The backdoor was open. You okay, man?"

"Uh. Yes." I say. "What are you doing here?"

"You said to come early. To get booze."

"Oh. Okay."

"You wanna go?"

"Uh. Yeah."

"You driving?"

"Can you?"

"Sure." Luke steps further into my room. Now I can see his furrowed eyebrows in the dim light. He is bending over and trying to look at me. I want to hide underneath a blanket. I want to crawl under into the smallest ball.

"You okay?"

"Yeah."

"Okay. Let's go."

The Ford Explorer rumbles. The vibrations feel good on my body. I think I feel better. Breathing is never easy, anyways. I want to thank Luke but I cannot talk and outside is dark and I'm locked in this tight car. Where are those streetlights? I don't like that the one above us is off. How long has it been here in the driveway? And the streetlight. It's supposed to be right above my driveway. I need to put music on. Should I ask him or just do it? Driving is making me sick. I cannot see anything on my phone. Who is coming later? Did we leave yet? Yeah. We are moving. My phone screen is blurring and swirling and it is glowing so much it hurts my eyes. I cannot type. Okay. Look up. Luke is driving. He does not look happy. Should I ask him what is wrong? No.

"Can we put music on?" I say. My voice is quivering.

"Yeah, sure. I got it."

Luke plugs in his phone. Tom Petty comes on. I like Tom Petty. Yes. I feel better now.

It is hard to look up. The horizon is deeply flat. Every single street light is fixed on a flat tableau sucking me in and the cars are all the same size, stuck, and the sky is a pale okra lined between all the objects and lines, I can see the lines who produce the world. Do not look at me.

"Where are we going?" I ask. My heart is beating. It is the only part of my body that I can feel.

My skin is unseen.

"Stop and Go."

"Why?"

"It's cheap. And they'll actually serve us."

"I do not want to go there."

I can exist. I can do it. I want to show Luke that I can handle this shit and walk in with him and he'll be floored. He'll tell everyone how cool I am.

"We have to, man. What did you want again?"

"Okay. We can. Beer."

"We can split something."

"Okay."

He is scaring me. The flat world is scaring me. The flat universe is scaring me. I am flat, compressed, barbed wire against the cement ground propelled through a flat reality I cannot look to my right or left but I can feel Luke right there. Right hand on the wheel. Shoulders leaning back. His left hand probably resting against his bottom lip. I can feel his right foot tapping against the gas in my stomach and his left tapping the flat plastic floor. In a flat plastic world. The gray streets. I cannot hear them. I close my eyes. Spinning colors. I open them. Flat world.

The car turns abruptly and bumps up a curb only to flatten white gravel. The car bounces around. He parks facing an old fence rusted along the edges and corners and bending like it is melting. I can't look at him. He says he'll be right back. I am quiet. My eyes are stuck. I close them. No more colors.

The fence is melting and bending over like a ruffled rose. But it is green. Like vomit with specks of plastic. In a fucking flat world. Car doors slam outside and reverberate through my skull and the sky is darker and darkening and I hear flip flops clacking and sneakers shuffling through the rock. I can turn my head. Okay. Dead grass grows at the bottom border of the melting fence. It is not melting now. It is just a bit bent by the wind. It is rusting and dying. Large weeds stick out from the border too. Not dandelions or creeping charlie. Tall stalks of sickly weeds. I hate those plants. What are they called? Oh, I don't remember. They smell so bad when you rip them out. And the juice leaks out and gets on your forearms and your little hairs get all matted down and. When was the last time I blinked? How long have I been in here? An hour? I'm here with Luke. I think. Where the hell is he? I hear the gravel crunching. Car doors slam. I can watch the traffic drive past. All the dim red lights and yellow headlights. Nothing like the colors in my head or the music in my ears. Music. It is silent in here. There are plastic bottles at my feet. Whenever I move my feet, I hear snaps of cheap plastic. How long has it been? I'm kicking my feet. I'm thrashing. My chest is tightening.

The car door opens and slams. Luke's eyes are wide. He pants a little bit. Shoves the beer into the back seat. Under the feet of an imaginary rider. Throws an old high school hoodie over the top and cranks the car into reverse and we fly backwards and I feel my shoulders smothered into the gray fuzz and the rough cushion and then my head jerks forwards as we drive out of the parking lot and back down the curbs and back out against the red and orange and gray flatness.

"Dude. Fuck that," says Luke. His eyes still panicked. My chest is still heaving.

"What happened?" I ask.

"These fuckin' guys. They were staring at me the whole time. I don't know... I think one of em' had a gun."

"In the store?"

"Yeah. In the store."

"Are you sure?"

"I mean, look around. Look at where the hell we are. You don't think it's a possibility?"

Why am I not scared? We cannot be here. I cannot be here.

"Oh, no."

"Yeah. I'm getting out of here. They might be following us," says Luke.

"Following us?"

"Yeah."

"Why?"

"I don't know… Cuz they want something." His eyes brows are digging into his eyeballs.

I am silent and I still see none of the strange things in the world the right way and my mind loops on questions that I don't have an answer to and I think I am smart but then I realize I am stupid and I should not think anymore but then I think I should think again and I am stuck in bed. Flushed down a black hole. But then I get a stupid idea.

"Do you think you died in there?" I say. I am confident for the first time in what I think are years, in all the time I saw the fence melting and the weeds growing.

Luke looks at me funny.

"What? No, dude. You okay?"

"Yeah."

"You sure?"

"You could have died."

"Yeah, I could have."

We are still driving fast back to my house.

"Okay... Think of this. Okay. Like what if you did actually die though and you're dead now?"

"I wouldn't be driving the car, dude." Luke laughs.

"But, what if I was just making this all up in my head? What if this was all a universe I had created in my head and I've died a million times and you have too and each death just makes a new universe that I keep creating in my head and I've been in a million car crashes but somehow the idea of living just keeps happening in my head?"

"Dude. What the fuck are you talking about?"

"Think about it!" Why am I confident? Do not be confident. Never be confident. Stop talking. "Like you died in there and a new universe was created to keep you alive and we're just in that one but in another universe you died in there and I'm sitting in the parking lot watching a fence melt for hours. Cause you were in there for hours. And they'd find me in there. The cops. Because they're always following. Like you said. And I'd be arrested and you'd be dead."

"You need a beer."

"I do..."

"Because that makes no sense at all."

"I know."

"You're lucky we're back." Luke stops and looks at me, grinning. It feels like hours. "And I guess I should tell you, I got your ass."

I am hardly awake now. I know I drank all the acid away. That's good. I was confusing myself. Now my friends are over. We're all having fun. I'm glad I drank the acid away. I am stumbling. I keep falling in a bush. I'm sorry. I keep breaking the flowers. Now my friends are standing in a circle throwing me back and forth like a rag doll. I can't stand. I just want to sleep.

Chapter 5 - I Feel Good and I'm Funny

I'm tweaking myself out here. I got scared, down there. I'm still me. I can see my hands and the lines of my palms. The police station would let me right in, scan my thumbs and tell me the correct answer.

I can't help myself from coming to the conclusion that being me doesn't change anything. I'll still be right here in the same spot. There isn't anything special about me. Or even good. Just a cog. Maybe that's a good thing.

Nope. I'm doing it again. I'm bringing myself down. I have to be more affirmative. I need to show the world I am a good person. I know I am. Deep down, I know just as much as the rest. I'm just as good as everyone else. I am a human and that's all I need to be good. I know you're gonna ask me what I mean by good. It's a good question. I think it's to help others. I know. I know. I just said I fucking hated everyone. I do. Why would I help others? There's a part of me that feels pity for everyone else. Just like I feel pity for myself. The other day, I was driving down the street and I saw a guy walking with his shoulders hunched over, carrying a bag of McDonalds. I felt bad for him. I wanted to cry and hug him. There was nothing wrong with him. I think that makes me a good person. I would've helped him.

And if that guy had let me talk to him, he would have liked me. The people I don't like are the ones who are dumb. They think they're right. They're all wrong. They regurgitate measurements. Guess what? My cock is fucking huge.

I don't know what I'm talking about.

Chapter 6 - Every Tree Is Going To Fall

This morning, it's raining. Last night, it rained too. The summer storms of Chicago. And it's all dark in my bedroom with the laptop droning on but the background sound of outside is much more pleasant. I like to feel comforted by the outdoors.

Mrs. O'Malley called. It's too wet outside and who knows how long it's gonna rain for. Take it easy today. But be ready tomorrow. The weather people are never correct, but I have a feeling it's gonna be hot. It's always hot.

What do I do? Guy is sleeping in the basement. This girl asked me if she could fuck him the other night. What kind of question is that? I don't have the answers. I doubt he wants to fuck her. Maybe they both know that. Then why ask? I wish someone would fuck me.

I'm hungry now. So I go downstairs and grab a carton of eggs, spinach, and mushrooms from the fridge. I crack two eggs into a plastic bowl and whisk them until they're a pale yellow slime. I'm trying to be healthy. I toss butter in the pan and spread it with a spatula. Perfect. I cut up an onion into short strands and toss them in with the mushrooms. I wait now. When they're both soft and when the kitchen is filled with a pungent odor I pour in the eggs and toss a handful of spinach on top. I wait until the eggs are cooked over and scramble everything. Then I scrape the food onto a plate and sit down. I forgot salt. Too late. I'm eating quickly. It's 9 A.M. and I'm starving.

I guess I can go workout. Nothing else to do in the morning. There is a blue mix in the cupboard that my dad uses. Two spoonfuls in a glass and add water. It makes my hands shake and bugs crawl under my skin. My eyes bulge and if I sit and wait I start itching at my fingertips and wrists. I lean over onto the table and my back arches and my spine pokes through my pale skin. I take too much. Otherwise I wouldn't exercise. I would sit and do nothing.

I like the tearing of my own muscles. It is difficult to convince yourself at first. But your mind realizes it needs to be punished. So, your body takes everything out on itself and you lift heavy things to destroy yourself on the inside and try not to think. The mind convinces itself that if you put yourself through the pain of destroying your own fiber you can look in the mirror and feel better about yourself when you have sex. So I like the pain. I like it when my body is telling me to stop and to give up and do nothing and sit and eat and jerk off but I tell it no. Most of the time I can't tell it no. I always want more. I can't help myself. But this is when I can truly hurt myself. And it becomes good. It is good when I can tell it no. And it is good to be in pain.

Sometimes I go into the garage without any music. That's where my dad set up the gym. He hates going to public gyms because there are other people there. I understand. I'm the same way. My pain is private. There is something about destroying yourself in silence that feels so good. You feel your body working and you hear the struggle in your winces. My winces are not very masculine. My dad's are. Mine aren't very loud either. My pain is private. Today is a day I go in without music. I am still confused about the acid and the flat world. I would like to forget but my mind won't let me. Maybe I will forget now. I don't get to choose what my mind will forget.

So here I am. Trying to pull myself up a metal bar hanging in a garage. Where did I find the idea that this would make anything better? I feel my shoulders struggling. I can only do two. It hurts as I look up to that metal bar but I can't see it when I get up there because my eyes are squeezed shut and I feel the pinch in the back of my shoulder muscles and they're rippling and not in the good way. The weak and sad way. I need to make it worse. I lay with my back on the bench. Overhead are the cork boards and weathered pine and it's dark and cramped and I can smell the rotting wood. Now, I let the metal bar come down to my chest. It weighs down on my heart and my ribs and I struggle to breathe when it rests there. Then I push it up. I feel the pinch and ripple in the corners of my chest muscles. It hurts. And I push. Over and over until I'm afraid the whole thing will fall on my head. I can picture this old wooden structure destroying itself. It only would if I was inside.

I go running now. I have music in my ears. The side of my calf muscles. The ones that are almost to the front of your leg. The ones on the outside. They hurt with every step. The tendon beneath my right foot is too tight and once I make it down the block it stings like a knife too. The oaks and maples speed over me and I stare at the sidewalk. I eat up and dodge the cracks and bumps and curbs. I don't want to fall. It would hurt and people would see me. I don't like it when people see me.

Guy is making breakfast. On the small table in the corner of the kitchen are stacks of paper and his laptop. That's not where we eat. A raised wooden block is in the middle of the kitchen connected to a wall and it faces the oven. Sliding doors flank the sides and we hide our plates and glasses there. Hanging on the white wall next to the island are all of my great aunt's pieces of work. Towards her later days, she began to draw. I don't know why she didn't start earlier. The pieces are wonderful. Many of them are abstract pastels of the French countryside or French ports. Their colors are bright and absurd. But there is one different piece. A pencil tracing of a woman. Her eyes are haunted and she stares through you. Her lines are faint and hollow. She is beautiful as she watches you everywhere you walk. I love her. I stare at her all the time. Then, I feel her eyes follow me and I get scared. She's always watching me.

I sit at the wooden counter below her and pour myself glasses of water that I gulp down until my throat is sore like the rest of my body. He is cooking bacon and the sizzling is loud. My chest doesn't hurt anymore. And she continues to watch us.

"You go running?" says Guy. I'm still panting. Sweat is dribbling down my face.

"Yeah. I almost went two miles today," I say.

"Two? I thought you were supposed to be in good shape." He laughs.

"Cigarettes don't help with that shit. My chest was on fire."

My face feels hot.

"I don't blame you. Same thing happens to me whenever I run. I don't run enough anymore."

"Nobody does."

"True. We're the worst... Well, just like everyone else. But honestly, you ever met someone way too into fitness?"

"Yeah."

"I hate those people."

"Everyone needs their thing, though."

"Not everybody needs to build their whole personality around one thing, though."

"That's true. I guess I kinda hate them too."

"You know, I might become one of them in L.A... Just to see how they tick."

"Like infiltrate them?"

"Yeah. Ironically, though."

"You're not gonna find what you're looking for, man."

"Why not?"

"People hide that shit."

Guy nods. We say nothing for a while, as the oil crackles over and over and the room gets warmer. His back is to me as he mindlessly plays with the bacon.

"What's your personality built around?" I say while staring at him. I haven't blinked for so long. And my face is still hot and red.

"I don't even wanna think about that," he says, shaking his head.

"Yeah..."

"That's why you don't look in the mirror on acid."

Guy pulls out a plate from behind the sliding glass which scrapes as it moves. Like grinding teeth. Bacon falls out onto his plate and it's dripping. I'm hungry again.

"You know, one time my friend got lost in the mirror on shrooms... I stared at a blinking light for a few hours so I didn't do much better," says Guy.

"I stared at a melting fence the other day."

"Oh, you tripped?"

"Yeah. I only took one."

"How much?"

"'Bout one-twenty-"

"Okay, good. You don't wanna over do it."

"I know. I have a system."

"When it comes to acid, there's not much of a system. You just do it."

"Yeah, but I like my system. I don't ever overdo it."

"Overdoing it is the shit. That's when you meet God."

"But does it ever make sense?"

He is silent for a while. "It feels like it."

I don't know what to say, so I nod.

"When are you gonna trip again?" he says.

"Probably at the end of summer, I guess... I need the occasion." I say.

"What about my birthday? It's at the end of summer and I'll probably move out after that. We can take a shit ton, smoke some weed and meet God."

I laugh. "That works in my system."

Inside a drawer in the wooden island, I find the baggie. A large tinfoil square wrapped around ten tabs of acid and caps and strands and bits of mushrooms floating at the bottom. Fifteen grams.

"How the hell are we gonna finish this all, though?" I say.

"We'll find a way-" says Guy. He is sitting next to me cutting his bacon now. An apple rests next to his plate. "We can always sell some of it."

"Okay." He turns his back so try to think of something to talk about. "How's the job search going?"

"It's good. The interview went pretty well. I'm hoping for a few more but I need to time them better. I can't always be flying out there."

"That's gotta be expensive."

"Oh yeah." He crunches into the apple. There is a layer of oil and grease lining his plate. It still smells so good. "I hate this weird persona I have to put on, though. I noticed it right away. My voice changed. My words changed... And when I was flying back here, I just laughed at it. That's all I could do."

"Why do you have to change like that? I like you the way you are."

"I don't know... But I really wanna move out there. I guess I have to."

"I understand. You gotta fit in to get the job." I shift around in my seat. "Guy... I think I wanna move too."

"Oh yeah? When are you thinking about doing that?"

"I don't know. After school probably."

"That's the best way to do it. Where to?"

"I don't know... L.A. would be cool."

"Oh, yeah. I mean you have the beaches, the weather. I'm so tired of the snow."

"Me too, man. I can't even picture it right now. Imagine wearing more than shorts and a t-shirt."

"I can't. And that's how you'll always feel in L.A. Unable to picture a winter coat." He laughs and I laugh too.

The shower is cool. I won't let it get hotter or colder. It's the right temperature. The sun is setting again. Guy is waiting for me to finish so he can shower. I should hurry up.

The sun sinks slowly. We are sitting around the kitchen island drinking beers and occasionally walking out to the back porch to smoke a cigarette. I think I'm going to take a quarter of a tab. Something to keep things interesting. I'm bored. There's so much so it's not a big deal. I'll be okay. It'll be fun. Fuck my system. I'm drunk.

I'm meeting my friends at the bar tonight. Guy is drinking with me but going to sleep soon. His laptop is glowing in the corner of the room. The pressure is wearing down on his shoulders. He's usually the happiest person in a room. Always has a joke. But he keeps looking over to that stack of papers and the demanding machine. He knows what he has to do. There can't be any fun tonight. But all my friends are at the bar and we all work together in the morning, so what's the difference?

The driveway is black. The streetlight is still out. No rapid blinking. No nothing. I am always afraid of walking down my driveway because I always think there's a raccoon hidden up in the tree waiting to pounce in the darkness. Something clawing into my back and digging its teeth into my neck leaving my wriggling and hurling as blood pools around me making my arms and legs warm and wet.

I guess I have to laugh at it. There's no way a raccoon would jump down and eat me. What kind of idiot am I? That doesn't happen. So I laugh. I'll do what Guy says. I'll laugh at the dumb shit my dumb brain comes up with.

I walk alone. Chicago is like every other place. It gets cool outside after the sun has gone. The only thing we can do is put up street lights. But I don't have one of those right now. A raccoon might sneak up and kill me. You never know.

I am in a t-shirt and shorts. I try to imagine a winter coat. That's when I begin to sweat. I am walking up the hill on 103rd and clutching a lone beer can which I bring up to my jaw and push my head back to drink. A pack of cigarettes is bouncing against my nipple in my pocket. I fiddle for one. The smoke is harsh at first but a mellowness flows into my body and I am excited to go to the bar. Nothing's going to happen. Just getting a couple beers. But I am pretty drunk. The acid is tapping at my back door. It doesn't want to be seen yet. I am okay with that. I don't want to meet it. Just chill.

I finish my beer and toss it to the curb. The busy street is within reach, I can hear it. I can't be drinking in public like that. So, I cross the street, empty handed, jogging a little bit, and looking over my shoulders. No cops. My hair is tinged with sweat in it, just like my t-shirt, which bounces against my damp skin. Sometimes it just sticks there.

The bouncer pulls the ID from my fingertips. Then he looks back at me and bends the plastic a little. Over his shoulder, I see my friends sitting at a circular table. Occasionally, someone will wave to one of them and they'll wave back as the rest sit. Nobody in this bar is 21. The bouncer is putting on a show. He hands back my ID and I walk to the table.

"Yo!" says Michael.

They turn to look at me and I'm smiling as I give them all handshakes. The bar itself is not big. It's never really crowded. Especially on a week day. Usually it's all old boozers and a few other people our age. But it's fucking packed tonight. It's making me nervous.

"What's the deal tonight?" I ask.

"Just get a bucket. You're not gonna find anything better." says Luke.

"Why are we here?" I ask and pause. "Why didn't we just go somewhere else? There's too many people around."

"This place is an institution, my man. It's a foundational element of our lives." says Michael, while laughing.

"Yeah, yeah. I know all that shit." I say. "But really?"

Michael shakes his head at me and raises his shoulders.

"I'm just gonna grab a bucket, then." I say.

A bucket of Miller.

The bartender nods.

He's just as bored as I am. Just like all the silent people standing around me. Down further, there's a guy flirting with a girl. She laughs and places her hand on his chest.

"Should we try somewhere else later?" I say.

"We can try. We just might not get in." says Luke. "And cheer up, dude. What's going on?"

"Nothing, you're right." I say. "I know, I don't wanna risk anything."

"Well drink up, man. You got here late." says Luke.

My eyes dart around a bit too much and my face is warming up. I need more booze in me. I chug one of my five.

Michael and Luke are sitting across from me. They're talking about something. I can't really hear them. Bob is on his phone next to me.

Luke taps me from across the table.

"Wanna hear what Michael just told me?" he says.

"What?" I say.

"He told me about this theory for the future. When the lower class is basically useless."

"Aren't they already useless?"

"Aww, you asshole. Tell him Michael."

Michael scoots his chair and clears his throat while laying his elbows down on the table.

"All right. So what's gonna happen, is when our virtual reality technology is good enough, we're gonna have to stick in all the unemployed motherfuckers. Cuz there aren't gonna be jobs for anyone, you know? Cuz of college being so goddamn expensive… And just everything being so god damn expensive. We have all these limitations. These ceilings. So we're gonna stick the poor people into these VR simulations. Basically from birth. And let them live out a hedonistic lifestyle…"

"Why?" I say.

"Cuz fuck em' that's why. I'm not gonna tell you why. I'm just telling you what it is!" says Michael.

"Wait. That sounds really familiar." I say. Luke is nodding and laughing.

"What? Is it your own life, you hedonistic motherfucker?" says Michael.

"That's gotta be it." I grab a beer from my bucket. "But seriously, what the hell is that?"

"You don't know?" says Bob finally. He's not even looking up from his phone. "Come on…"

"Nope… I don't." I say.

"It's fuckin' Matrix…" says Michael.

"What? Aww, you assholes." Luke and Michael are laughing while cradling their beers to their chests.

"I was picturing something different. Something happier, maybe." I say

""What? Just constant masturbation?" says Michael.

"Jesus." says Luke.

"I don't know. Maybe something fulfilling." I say.

"Yeah? Fulfillment? Fuck outta here with that idealistic bullshit." says Michael while laughing. "We're here to live and die."

"Then why not speed up the process?" I say.

"What? Cuz suicide can't be fun-" says Luke. "You wanna try it and tell us all about it?"

"What about making life a little bit easier then." I say. "I mean, Jesus Christ…"

"That's never gonna happen. And your life's not even that bad. It's good." says Michael. He looks around the bar. "I mean look at all these cops in here. And future cops. These are the motherfuckers that decide your fate, if you let them. And you know how they got there?"

"How?" I say.

"By realizing they had no other choice."

"So it's simple. I like that. Why don't I just become a cop?" I say.

"Come on... You? A cop?" All my friends laugh. I laugh too.

"Yeah. And cops are assholes anyways." says Michael.

"Fuckin' narcs-" I say. "Probably the worst people."

I trail off and look around the bar. Still snakes of people maneuvering in the tight space between the tables and the bar.

A hand taps my shoulder. I turn around.

"Hey, buddy." says a man. He must be 27 years old with a tight black beard and a tight shirt. It reads the bar's name locked inside a CPD crest. His forearm was folded over the back of his chair and it is bulging with muscle. There wasn't much hair left on the top of his head and his jaw was clenched.

"What are you guys talkin' about over here?" he says.

"Nothin'. Just ragging on cops." I say. I'm laughing. I feel better now, after some beer.

He looks at me with a blank stare but there is a note of intensity in his widened pupils.

"You're gonna tell me that, buddy? What do I look like?" he says.

My friends are silent.

"I don't know." I say.

"I'm a cop. I thought we were on the Southside. Where you respect cops."

"Yeah. I mean we're just joking around."

"You know what? If the jokes were funny I'd laugh but you guys are all retards."

I don't know what to say. I'm gaping like a fish. I don't know what to say.

"I mean, I'm sorry, man." I finally whisper.

"Don't call me "man". You can't call me man until you're a man. How old are you? 15?"

"I'm 21."

"Yeah. We'll see about that."

The man stands up and calls over to the bouncer. I feel my face red now. My stomach is squirming. The bass is pounding in my chest. There's the bouncer. He's walking over. Everyone has to be watching.

"Get this asshole outta here." he says to the bouncer.

The bouncer nods and points to the door. I tell him I have more beer left. He grabs my shirt collar and begins to drag me. I tell him it's cool. People are staring. He doesn't let go and drags me across the floor, snaking through the crowd milling about. I feel their breath and their eyes. At the door, he tosses me by my collar. I fall onto the pavement and stand up quickly and scurry around the corner into the alley, like a cockroach. My stomach is sick and I feel tears welling in my eyes.. I'm not gonna cry. Stop. I cry too easily. Shut up. I check my phone. I send a text. I beg them to meet me. Please come outside, I just want to be drunk.

I don't know who that guy is. Maybe he does shit like this over and over to guys like me. I want to go back in there and punch him in the face. But I would never be able to. I say I can. But my back is against the brick wall in the alley next to this stupid bar and I'm sucking down a cigarette. I want the smoke to sting my lungs. I want my head to feel weightless like a black balloon.

In my mind, I can feel the pressure of his cheekbone against my knuckle. I can hear it too. There is nothing I want more right now than to see the skin along his cheek tearing. I want to see his blood. I want him to feel my face with the back of his hand and see just a speck of blood squirting into the air so he can smirk at me and put his hand around my throat and punch me in the nose. I want him to toss my head into the brick wall so it can be weightless like a black balloon.

Voices are calling for me. My eyes are closed and I'm on a third cigarette.

"Fuck that guy. That's why you don't wanna be a cop... I think your dick automatically shrinks into a nub." says Michaelr.

Luke taps my shoulder and I hand him a cigarette.

"Chode." I say.

"Yeah. Who is that guy?" Says Luke.

"I don't know," says Michael.

"I wanna know." I say. "I wanna know who that guy is." But I'm all talk. I know I am. I think they know I am.

I walk back to the front of the bar. He's sitting there with his buddies. They're laughing. All of their faces are cooked up with scraggly beards crawling like worms. They're the insects. Not me. He looks up and sees me. He winks.

Fuck that guy. I light up another cigarette and walk back to the alley where my friends still are. I tell them we need beer and to go to my house and we need to let people know they should come over.

I don't like to think about things like surgery. Picture this. A serrated knife moving slowly through the thin flap of skin holding the yards of intestines in your stomach. If they were ever to spill out they'd wriggle around like a big worm. It's moving slowly through you and all you can do is lay there and wait. But I can picture that cop's stomach being slowly sliced open. God. It makes my skin tingle.

Everyone's here now. I see all my friends. I am standing in the middle of my kitchen in front of the island and all my friends are circled around it too. I see Michael, Bob, Luke, Duffy, Jay, Chloe, Jenna, Chris, Carley, Riley, Mike, Bill, Barry. I see Melinda, Molly, Mike again, Dan, Joshua, Tom, John, Matt, Tim, Ava, Mark, Erin, Martin, Donald. Mike, Mike, Mike. The names all sound funny in my head. What do I do with such a strange group of people? What do we do with such strange definitions?

There's a deck of cards sprawled across the wooden table and people are slamming their drinks against the wood or chugging them and letting the booze spill down their chins and the wood is getting sticky and the cards are sticking to the wood. Everyone is laughing. Good. Oh, it's my turn.

"You always go with your heart." I say.

My fingers try to grab the edge of the card but it's slippery. An Ace of Diamonds. The rest of my beer goes down my throat as everyone laughs at me and I go get another from the fridge. One by one we recite our little doctrine. Some find their heart and others finish their drinks. But then we collect the cards and shuffle them back up. Around the table we go guessing the nature of our cards. I guess it is a stupid game. But every game is stupid when you think about it.

Hours later, we are on the cement basketball court with a floodlight pointed at the exposed brick of my house shining a white light up into the night. A large black speaker sits in a bed of gravel and we are playing loud music. We are all sweaty and drunk. Duffy is yelling and spinning and looks like he has forgotten what it is to be human. He looks like a spinning top.

All of a sudden, a loud crash erupts. It must have been a car crash. But it couldn't. The ground shook. The ground doesn't shake during car crashes. We all rush through the gate.

A large oak tree is laying across the street. A car is crushed beneath it. The roof smothered and the windshield shattered and pieces of metal and plastic and glass are spattered along the road. Tree branches sprawling out like a meteor crash. And leaves fluttering about in the golden light.

Crowds of my neighbors are standing about. Everyone is circling the accident one by one walking afraid to speak. Then we are brought together. Faces are incredulous or laughing. My friends are laughing and gasping. I see Duffy walk around to the other side of the tree and he's speaking with a group of my neighbors. People I had never even seen before.

"How does a tree fall?" I ask Jay.

"Beats me, dude." He says while sipping his beer in the middle of the street. His mouth scrunches to the side. "I can't believe I just said that."

"You think someone was out here chopping it down?" I say.

"We would've heard it."

"True."

We both laugh.

"I hope that's not someone's car from here."

"Yeah. Cuz if it's not, who gives a fuck."

"Good point."

Headlights light up the tree and a car is coming towards us from the west. I am standing almost next to the trunk now assessing the damages and feeling the grooves in the tree. I wave to the car. The man driving looks at me and then the tree. He makes a strange face and rubs the bottom of his brown beard with his hand. I wince. I turn around.

"Okay, everyone! Back to the yard."

They herd themselves to the backyard and the music continues to ring throughout the night. I follow behind in silence. I feel strange. Where the hell is Guy? I need to ask him something.

Chapter 7- I'm a Child

Maybe everyone else does like me. Maybe I just do like everyone and nobody ever learns a god damn lesson. Most of it's all an accident. You know what? Everything's an accident. The only reason I'm alive is because of an accident. I haven't talked to my parents in weeks. And it's a complete accident. Yeah. Everything's an accident. And that's why you can't be rational. You find shit that makes sense to you and you follow it. That makes sense.

Are you bored? I'm just rambling- I promise there's a point.

I guess I'll tell you about school. I'm good at talking about that. Stacks of bleached blocks. Wooden frames etched around metal doors. Numbers for everyone. Showers clogged with sperm. My week-old orange vomit sprayed on bathroom tile. Every Wednesday it was removed and replaced. Everyday I closed my eyes and raised my chin into the steaming water and let it drip down my whole body as I tugged to whatever popped into my brain. Most of the time it was a black screen.

My bedroom. Jesus Christ. Clothes all over the place. Tiles glued to the floor, and then unstuck. My bare feet coated in the sticky shit. Empty bottles of booze stacked like trophies. I liked how disgusting it was. It made me feel better. My roommate moved out after the first semester. We were both assholes. I was a scumbag and he was pretentious. That's okay. He joined a fraternity. So I took his bed and slid it against mine and threw the rickety wooden frames against the wall closest to the window and I had my ashtray and my bowl right there. Smoke before bed. It helped. My mini-fridge was underneath that mess. I spilled milk in it the first week of school. Didn't use it after. It didn't smell. I drank vodka. Sometimes alone. Then I knocked on doors in that fortress. Those blank white walls. I knocked on those doors and ran away. I was at the wrong door blacked out once thinking it was my own. I pounded on the door for two hours. It hurt. I remember it bruised the bottom of my fist.

Nevermind. I don't even wanna talk about school. I hope you understand. No, it sucks. You're right. I should. I need to. I need to change. I can't be me anymore.

There was one place. An angled hallway with a blue ceiling and one blue wall. The wall facing the outdoors was orange glass. The corridor was 10 feet long and the men's bathroom was halfway along the blue wall. Warm light came in and lit up the orange wall and cast a pale coral shadow against the blue floor late in the afternoon. I walked there every day for that.

But there came a time when I didn't. Where there was only darkness in my room. I didn't drink. I didn't smoke. I didn't do much of anything- Shut up. You're not a therapist. I know that's what you think. I'm weak. I'm not. Don't tell me that.

Why am I even talking to you? I don't even know what the fuck you are. I don't wanna talk about that. Stop looking at me.

Chapter 8 - Time Passes

I am back at the wooden slab. The salmon is laying on the grill outside on a bed of lemon juice and herbs inside an aluminum foil casing. Smoke rises. I don't know the salmon. I don't even know where he came from. He is big and strong but I've never seen him swim.

The french doors behind me are open and the smell of cooking fish mixes with the old beer dried on the kitchen table. The smell of the alcohol floats up from the cans that I pushed to one side of the table. I am in the seat closest to the wall, hidden in my corner away from all those cans and bottles. The woman in the drawing sits above me. Her blackened eyes burrow into the top of my head. Like the sun when I work outside.

A timer goes off. The worst sound in the world is an alarm. I will eat the salmon with a side of raw spinach.

The salmon is good. I leave my plate in the sink and wrap up the rest and place it in the fridge next to the assortment of leftover beers. Busch, Miller Lite, Rolling Rock, PBR, Milwaukee's Best, Piss.

The blue powder is like sand mixing with water but it goes down and makes me itchy. My wrists and fingers are tingling and the skin below my eyelid hurts.

The sun is on my head now. My calves hurt less. I run through the neighborhood.

On top of the hill, two blocks from my house are large mansions. I never see anybody go in or out of them. There is a certain moment I relish. I don't care about their beauty. I don't like looking at them. But when a friend from far away comes, I sometimes take them down the street so they notice them. And I smile and feel good inside. That's why I look at them when I run past. Now my calves hurt and my skin shrivels and I feel bad and I feel pain.

The trees are beautiful as they hang over the skinny side streets. Over the hill and past the mansions are houses just like mine and I see people parking their cars or sitting on their stone porches and I hear basketballs bouncing and kids shouting.

I make a rectangle and I almost trip running over the train tracks. A bell is ringing after I cross. I can feel the gates closing slowly behind me and the train rumbling through. My friend told me a story once. She knew a girl whose foot got stuck when she was crossing the tracks and a train hit her. A big metra. Dead instantly. Then I read a story in the paper about a kid who drank too much at one of the bars and fell asleep on a set of tracks. Right by us. Dead instantly. Sometimes I'm surprised I'm not dead. Sometimes I wish it would end like that.

Guy is making food. He looks bored. I'm bored. The stack of papers and the laptop are still sitting on the side table but they're on top of layers of paper towels since that table is sticky and smelly too.

"Any luck?" I ask as I sit down in my usual chair.

He smiles. "Getting there. I have a couple phone interviews today. I've gotta warm up. Remember what it's like over there."

"Good luck." I say without any other special words. I wish I could talk like him. I wish it was easy like that.

"Yeah. It's not like an internship. You've had one of those right? You know how it only takes one interview to get one? And they're important to have. But they don't care about those anymore. They don't really care about school. It takes two or sometimes three interviews to convince them to meet you."

"And you're all the way in Chicago."

"That's the only problem"

He turns back to his pan and the sizzling grows louder. My fingers dance along the table like little caterpillars.

"What kind of jobs are you looking for?" I ask.

"Oh. Something in IT, right now. I don't know if that's what I want to do though."

"Why not?"

"I don't want to be stuck in the city forever. Or in computers. I'd rather do something outside in nature. "

"Is that even possible nowadays? I don't think you can really be a farmer anymore. I guess you can be a fisherman."

"You can't do that in L.A. Maybe I can find something at the state parks out there. I don't know. I need to get out there first. And out of I.T."

"Why are you getting in, then?"

"Gotta start somewhere."

"I don't know what I wanna do."

"It doesn't matter. It really doesn't. The only thing that matters is how you look and if you can talk well. That's all that matters."

"So I'm screwed."

"Nah. Not yet."

"Why not?"

"Cuz you can change into what they want."

"I guess."

"Wanna hear what I think?"

I nod.

"You take it like me. The second I get out there, I'm going to attach myself to something. Something I really want. I don't know what yet. But I'm going to find something to stick to. Something in nature. Like Big Sur. Maybe a park ranger." says Guy.

"I thought those jobs were really hard to get. I think they fill up fast. They might not be hiring, man."

"They will be. And I'm a good interviewer. You just talk like them." •

"How?"

"You just say the right words." He laughs a little. "You've gotta get out of here. You need to see California. That's where you discover things. Since I've been there, I've been discovering so much."

"Like what?"

"I realized how ugly I was."

"Is that why you don't look in the mirror on acid?"

"No. I just realized how old I looked out there. My skin has all these scars on it from when I had pimples. I've gotta look younger."

"But you look good."

"Not to their standards."

"But who cares?"

"They do, man. You've gotta look good to feel good!"

"I guess I'm kinda ugly too, huh?"

"Yeah. But you can change that! Laugh at yourself a bit, man."

"What's the point of that? It's not funny. And it really doesn't change anything."

"Yeah it is. It's funny that you're ugly. It's funny that I'm ugly. They'll laugh at us too. And if everyone's laughing, then what does it matter?"

"I don't get it."

"You would. Out there."

The food is done and Guy is losing interest. I know. The woman is still staring down at me.

"When are your friends gonna be here?" I ask.

"Uhhh, two weeks-" says Guy.

"We're gonna throw them a big party?" I say.

"That's your call."

"Yeah, we will. It's not like people haven't been here."

"Yeah."

"I better hide some stuff. I keep thinking people are gonna take shit."

"That's a good idea."

Guy is eating in front of his laptop. I sigh and walk upstairs and close my bedroom door and drapes. I jerk off and nap. It feels good.

Later, Guy pulls out the baggie from its hiding spot in the drawer in front of the seat I usually sit in.

"You wanna take a small dose?" says Guy.

"Ehh... I don't think I should." I say. "Been taking way too much acid."

"C'mon. Have you taken shrooms before?"

"Nah... But my system-"

"Fuck your system. Take a little bit. Try mine out"

"Okay."

"You're easily convinced."

I chew one cap slowly. It tastes rancid. But I swallow with a big gulp.

The dog is wagging his tail at the front door and barking in the direction of his leash. He knows we are going on a walk. I think it's everyone's favorite time of day. I'll say it over and over.

Outside, we face west. There is a small clearing in the middle of my street, an opening in the canopy of tall oaks and maples. The sun is dripping down the flattened sky. The cirrus clouds are magenta. It is so beautiful. Guy has a large smile on his face and we're standing in the middle of the concrete clearing. The dog paces around us. Sniffing the air.

The sidewalk wiggles below my feet and every color is beautiful. I feel a bulge in my throat when the lights from the street lamps turn on.

The dog jogs ahead with a lifted nose and breathes in the air of today. Right now. Then he stops when a plot of grass interests him and I have to yank him gently. Why do I need to? Next time I'll forget and we'll stand still for a very long time.

"How are you feeling?" asks Guy.

"I'm feeling good. You?" I say.

"Me too."

There's not much to say. We're in the sidestreet grid of Beverly. That's that.

"I keep saying this, man..." says Guy.

"This is the best time of day?" I say.

"Nah. I'm just really excited for L.A."

"You think it's gonna happen?"

"Yeah."

There are no cars and there is no background noise. It is just us two in this entire world. We are standing on a corner next to a mailbox but somehow this is the most important place my two feet have ever been. At the same time, this is every day I've ever experienced. The absurdity of it all. I have been in this spot, and the sky has been this beautiful, I have been this happy, a million times before. I always want to feel like this.

"I wanna go to L.A." I say.

"Yeah? Why?" says Guy.

"I want to get there because I don't wanna be here."

"Why is that?"

"Because I'm tired of being here."

"But you can't move yet."

"Why not?"

'Because you've got school to finish."

"Why can't I just go anyway?"

"Because you need to finish school. It's kinda like a ritual. You need to wait for the next one."

Guy is walking ahead of me and his right hand is resting on the dog's head. The dog is happy and so are we. It is good, right now.

I want to go to L.A.

"Listen, man. You don't wanna go to L.A." says Guy. "Not right now."

Then we are silent.

"I have a funny story." I say.

"Yeah?" says Guy.

"I got kicked out of a bar the other night."

"Yeah? Why?"

"Cuz I said mean things about a cop."

"What cop?"

"I don't know... Some guy sitting behind me."

"And he kicked you out?"

Guy begins to laugh as we stumble along.

"Yeah."

I am laughing too.

"What an asshole!" says Guy.

"I hate him." I say.

"Know what I would do if I was a cop?"

"What?"

"I'd kill myself."

We watch TV until the waves are gone and the tide is slow and the water of our vision is smooth like the summer night. I feel so empty.

Now I am wandering the dark streets alone. There are no squirrels, or birds, not even raccoons. The cars are sleeping, too. The wind blows lightly, and I hear the leaves above my head rustling.

I am swallowed by a trance, dictated by the sounds of cicadas and rubbing leaves and the pale glow of golden lights.

I am so empty and alone, on the grid-like streets.

So I find myself on the corner of 103rd and Western and look over to the bar.

It makes me sick, its silence. I turn around and fall back into my comfortable, mindless, trance.

And I realize, nothing is ever going to happen to me.

Chapter 9 - There is Never Time to Talk

I wish the light would leave me alone. The darkness of a cavern. Yes. I hear them talking over in their corner of the backyard. By the gray plastic fence stuck in the muddy mulch. By the slanting garage. Their voices are soft and far away and I am just on my knees in the mud. They talk about interesting things.

Michael is laughing and a shovel is stabbing the damp earth.

"I can't believe that, dog!" yells Michael.

"Man... Why do you always say that? Nobody says that around here." says Luke.

"What? Dog?" says Michael.

'Yeah, dumbass."

"Cuz you're a bitch. That's why!"

I want them to talk more about the matrix or how fun last night was or stories from college. I just want to listen.

The dandelions are much smaller today. The mud covers them up and their stems are slick with dew. The Creeping Charlie is completely submerged and my knees feel wet. I play with every worm I find. They are thin and tender and moist. There was one that I cut in half and then I started doing it to all of them as my mind drifted away listening to them talk. I can't hear Bob.

"Is Bob here?" I yell into the ground.

"What?" says a voice.

"Is Bob here?"

"Oh. Yeah, he is. You need help?"

"No. It's okay."

"Okay."

"All right. So have you seen the movie Flight?" says Michael.

"Nope." says Luke.

"Well, it's with Denzel Washington. As an alcoholic pilot. How funny is that?"

"I'd have to see it to tell you."

"Listen, man. He's got his shit straight, okay? He isn't drinking anymore but towards the end of the movie, he has to do this big flight."

"A big flight?"

"Yeah. A big flight."

Michael and Luke carry on. My hands continue working in the mud.

"So yeah. He gets nervous or some shit. And gets hammered. Like absolutely fucked up. He can't even walk. But he's got this big flight, you know?"

"Yeah."

"So fuckin'... What's his name. Yeah. John Goodman hands him a cigarette dipped in blow. And he goes. Here man, smoke this coco puff. You'll feel better."

"Coco puff?"

They are both laughing hard and the laughter is bouncing from plastic fence to wooden wall to my ears. I guess I'm laughing too. I think so.

"A fuckin' coco puff!" says Michael.

I could use a smoke. I look down at my hands. They are trembling and all covered in mud. All the way past my wrists. A circle of worms wriggle around my bucket. All cut in half wriggling in opposite directions. Squirming in the moisture like little centipedes. My stomach feels sick. There are so many. Nobody can see this. It's weird. I pick up the worms one by one and they squirm in between my index finger and my thumb and I toss them in the bucket. They are a fine layer above the weeds and mud so I dump some grass and stand up. My knees are brown.

"Anybody know where the hose is?" I call out.

"Yeah. Back of the house against the wall." says Bob.

"Thanks. I need a drink."

My bucket is heavy with mud. I carry it to the garbage can and dump the contents out. I put it down and walk to the hose. I could have just found it myself. I didn't have to involve them in my bullshit.

Above the hose is a large window into the kitchen. I stare inside as I let the water run over my hands.

A man with a brown beard walks to the sink and turns on the faucet. I can't hear it but I can see him running his hands beneath the water, too. He looks familiar. His hat is pulled down in front of his face. I know the profile. Who the fuck is that guy? I spray my knees with the hose and I feel the water running down my calves into my socks and boots.

The man turns to look at me outside. I know him. I definitely know him. I walk back to the corner where my friends are.

"Guys. Guess who's in the house." I say.

"Who? The old lady? Who gives a shit-" says Michael.

"Nah. What old lady?"

"It doesn't matter, man..." Michael laughs as he trails off. "Who's in there?"

"The cop from the other night." I say.

"Wait. No way." says Luke. "There's no way."

He begins to laugh.

"No, really. He's in the kitchen. Go check him out." I say.

"No. That's weird-" says Luke.

"I'll go." says Michael.

We watch him trudge through the yard onto the cement patio and to the window. He turns and shakes his head.

"You liar." he says, while laughing.

"No, I'm serious!" I say.

"Well, who cares? What are you gonna do?" says Luke.

"Nothin'."

"Exactly."

"It's hilarious, though" says Michael.

"We should egg his house." I say.

"Dude. How old are we?" says Luke.

"Not old enough to drink according to this cunt." I say.

"Wanna go tell him that?" says Michael.

"Nah." I say.

I want to hurry up and finish our job. I don't want to see him again.

At home, I ask Guy if he wants to smoke. He looks up quickly and says yeah. Then his eyes focus back down. Gimme one second, he says.

There is a door upstairs in my house that leads to the back rooftop. The house is strange. But we roll the blunts upstairs in my bedroom littered with dirty clothes and blunt wrappers and beer cans. I am nervous. I don't think my friends care but it smells bad here. So I ignore it as my face burns up. When the blunts are rolled, we open the door and go sit on the roof. We are all muddy and the sky has turned from gray to sunny and I feel good about the sun now.

Michael, Luke, Bob, and I. There are beach towels laid out on the gray shingling. Otherwise it's too rough. I find beer cans scattered across the roof and one stuck in the gutter. There is the skylight. I look through the window and Guy is sitting quietly at the laptop. I stare. He doesn't move. Only his fingers show any signs of motivation. I think he has too many jobs to apply for. It's all he cares about now. It's not like I don't want him to get a job. I don't like him the day he comes back from L.A. And he's always there. I like it better when he doesn't care about that. I like it when he cares about me and getting fucked up.

We sit cross legged in a circle. Michaelr plays music from his phone and passes the flame from a lighter up and down the blunts. My hips hurt from sitting cross legged so I lay down on my side. But the rough shingling scrapes my skin. There is no feeling comfortable.

"You know what?" says Michael.

"What?" says Bob.

"This is it right here. This is one of those moments."

"What kinda moment?" I say.

"One of those moments I look around and say to myself, what did I do to deserve all of this kindness. Look around."

He was right. The sun is edging downwards to the west and breaking the planes of green leaves and creating the golden light you see from time to time. The light is spreading its warmth through all of the backyards and the leaves shudder in the wind. We sit above it all, stinking.

Michaelr takes one blunt and Luke the other. They light the ends and we start smoking. I don't know what music Michaelr is playing.

I see the vines coiled around my tree below us in the backyard. The strangling ivy. My mother is growing vines to wrap around our back deck and onto this strange structure my dad and I built. It's only 4 posts stuck into the ground, and four other posts connecting those posts. My friends laugh at it. But the vines give it character. They're not alive yet. I don't know if I like vines or not.

There's too much silence. I look around and see the light coming down. The wind blows softly. But my mind continues. It won't ever stop. I can think about thinking and about my thoughts and then it always falls back on me. It's always bad. I don't like that. I want to see what's wrong with the world. With others.

"What do we usually talk about here?" I say.

"I don't know… Bullshit." says Luke.

They all laugh.

"It don't matter, brotha." says Michael as he hits the blunt. "Language is all a lie, anyways..."

"Jesus Christ, Michael. You're all over the fuckin' place today. I don't think you've said one that makes sense." says Luke.

"That's what I do." he says.

Bob is lightly toking the blunt and staring up into the sky. The breeze passes through and everything is still once again. I can't stop staring at the golden mist. And the rough, constricting, square, grid-like, plots of land, defined by the sharpest, most constricting lines. All hiding behind that perfect, golden light.

Then the blunt is passed to me. I always forget the taste and feeling. The smoke grows in my chest after I let it out like a bubble and suck it back in. A girl told me it looked cool once, so I do it every time. The weed is different.

"What is this?" I say. It tastes strange-

"Not sure. I got it from a friend. I think it's from Colorado or California."

"Am I gonna be okay?" I ask.

"Yeah. Why wouldn't you? You've been taking acid like every day." says Luke.

"I don't know… You sure?"

"Yeah."

"You guys aren't tricking me or anything?"

"No. Relax. It's all good, man."

It feels different to me. I don't know. I don't know why it feels so much different right now. I can feel time slowing down slightly and the world becoming brighter. In a blinding way.

"I'm gonna grab some water. Anyone want anything?" I say, talking as slowly as possible. I don't want my voice to be affected.

"Nah, I'm good." They all say. More or less.

It's okay. The shingling is gritty below my feet. I should've worn shoes. God, I am naked. And I am empty. The walls in the hallway seem to shrink around me as I walk through. It's okay. It's dark inside the house. My eyes are adjusted to the sunlight. My legs feel shaky.

In the kitchen, I slide open the glass door and pour myself a glass of water. Guy looks up from his laptop.

"You okay? You look weird." he says.

"Yeah." I say. Very slowly. I stop. I look at him.

"What's L.A. even like? I've never been there."

"I know you haven't." Guy shuts his laptop and with a half smile, looks up at the white ceiling.

"Sit down, dude. I'll tell you."

You fly in. There's a lot of people at the airport and everybody walks around like they're important. So, you feel important. I used to laugh at people like that. But you get there and you're walking around with a bunch of people with a raised chin, and you feel yourself doing it too. And when I live there, I'm not gonna do that. I don't know if I'll be able to escape the feeling, though. I'm not gonna be that. But you walk outside and you see the palm trees and the air is light and the sun is shining. There's this fuckin' energy you don't get anywhere else. Like, man. This is it. This is it right here. I go to the beach and see the girls and drive through Hollywood, and I'm like damn. This is it. This is me, now. I wanna be a part of this big idea.

His eyes are beaming as he stares at the ceiling still. I just feel her eyes on the back of my head.

And you know what? I haven't even been there that long. And I can already tell. They just live differently. They're ahead of the world. Their values are better than ours. You know? Every

77

person needs values and the ones you learn here are bad. Chicago is too classic. It's old school. I don't want to be like that anymore. I want to laugh at shit. I want to be in the moment! I want to be in that moment. I want people to see me and say, damn, that guy is in the moment. Their rules are just different, man… It's like there aren't any. Except the ones that are there.. Are just good… You know? They're good rules. I want those rules. And I want to be in those moments. But I'm still funny. You know? And you know what L.A is? A place for rebirth. Not just for me or you but everything, man.

Chapter 10 - I Hate You

I can't believe how uniform it can all be. Nobody wants to hear anyone pound on the door when it's 5 AM. Letting them know they've gotta go do something they don't wanna do. But millions of other people do that shit every day. Why would I wanna be another person to subject himself to such an unnatural life?

The world is a lot like a coach. A bad one. A coach who sells you shit. An unfair coach. One who looks you in the eyes and explains it's all a life lesson and you get bitched at sometimes and you're only allowed to follow a strict code of rules they have decided. And I committed to this code of rules without any kind of consent. But I did kind of consent? That's what you're saying. At what point does consent begin, and when does a human consent after they have understood a shit experience awaits them. And what causes me to continue through with that experience, with full consent, knowing I will suffer. I will lay on a bed of nails, tears will bubble in the corners of my eyes, and I will be showered with unearthly gifts. Yes, when the suffering ends, it will be heaven. The fucking garden. Now, that is why we suffer. And that is why I love to suffer. Yeah. That's what you're thinking. Jesus Christ. Am I a masochist? I know. I think I know. I will wait for my gifts, the ones I deserve for being me. For being so special. For being the only person on Earth with these kinds of bubbles in my eyes. The only one with a brain so great. How could I continue with those thoughts in my head? So, me, the world's smartest man, then realizes how wrong I am. So I stay on my bed of nails, with my tears in my eyes, and I laugh my laugh. I laugh at the world, and I laugh at those who think anything will ever come to them. I wait.

Because I am a human, I will never feel an ounce of gratitude. When I lay a bed of nails and I am showered with gifts, wouldn't I make the logical choice of getting up and finding another bed of nails to wait on? And again, I don't know what choice is. I often think about that. My entire life has been determined for me. Now what?

Yes, I know. I must take responsibility for my choices. Even if they weren't mine. What if I make the wrong choice every time? Is it because I'm always given the two wrong choices? Am I not smart enough? It can't be me. But when I look out to the world, I see millions of people luckier than me and smarter than me and more attractive than me and with better lives than me. And then that fucking tick comes. The me, me, me, me. The index finger digging around my belly button. Me. And what about the set of choices I was given? Are they not good enough? Surely, they must be.

So if there's nothing wrong with me or my life, it must be something else. I think it's you. You haunting me like this. Reading every thought and judging me. No. It's the world's set of choices. You do this, and you do that. Make me your perfect little robot, world. I will be your perfect little robot. Just give me a choice to be good. See, I grew up without religion. I just need someone to give me the choice.

Chapter 11- Fun Party

Fucking Guy. He's too fast. I can't keep up with him anymore. He's three of those sidewalk squares ahead of me and with every block, he gains separation. My chest hurts again. It always will. I can feel my hair bouncing on my head and slapping my shoulders. I should get it cut. Now, he's four squares ahead of me. I'm trying so hard to pick up the pace. My calves hurt. My shoulders swing side to side, my face strains into an ugly grimace, and I can hear the scraping of my shoes on the cement.

I don't want to anymore. I just want to stop and never have to run again. It's unbearable.

The water is leaking onto my face. It is warm and relaxing. The overhead fan is on, buzzing along like a lonely fly. The water dropping onto the plastic shower curtain, clicking. The room heater on the other side of the marble wall. It's all so warm and friendly. I try not to let my phone get wet. It's in my left hand and I'm trying to swipe with my thumb but it's too short. There we go. It's disgusting that I do this but I have to. The woman is not real. Her tits look like they're going to explode. Her thighs are like chopsticks. Ass like a lollipop. How much did she pay? For a while it works. Then I close my eyes and try to picture anything else but it's a black screen. It always is. My dick is getting soft. Hurry. My chest is seizing up. My shoulder is sore. Hurry. Who's that in my brain? No. I look back at the fake woman. It all comes out from me and goes straight down the drain. My head is spinning and I have to put my hand against the marble wall. I'm panting and dizzy. The steam burns. Fuck. I'm so empty.

The towel is coarse on my body. I'm pretty sure it's old. Somebody was using it to mop up beer off the floor the other night. I threw it into the hamper and now it's coarse.

I'm dry now. What to do. I'll watch TV. I don't really want to, but there isn't anything to do until later. Luke is throwing a big party. I love his parties. All my friends are going. And Luke's brother will be there again and he's bringing all of his friends. He's a nice guy. He moved away from Chicago after school. Lucky bastard. But I haven't talked to him in a long time.

Guy is sitting next to me. Our legs are resting on the wooden coffee table and we crack open beers because we are bored.

"Should we take the acid tonight?" I say.

"I don't think I'm gonna." says Guy.

"Why not?"

"We've been tripping a lot, man. What happened to your system?"

"You made me take shrooms the other day. Remember?"

"You did that yourself."

"And it's just acid. Not coke or anything."

"That's almost worse. That's why I say fuck your system"

"Then why shouldn't I take it? You're the one who said I should be overdoing it."

"I don't know, man... Maybe you need another system."

"Like what?"

"I don't know- Stop asking me all these questions. You're gonna have to figure that shit out yourself-"

"I'm sorry." I pause. "It's not like I'm gonna get addicted or anything."

"I don't know. You might."

"I'm gonna take some."

"You sure?"

"Yeah."

"All right then."

Guy sighs and looks back up to the TV. His shoulders slouch.

The beer tastes good even though it's piss water. It's Busch.

I'm scrolling through the channels. We don't know what to watch. My thumb is a robot clicking on buttons. I leave an old preacher's show on for a while. I wonder how much money he spends on public TV for no one to watch. The only people who watch are those making fun of him like me and Guy. I want to picture his life.

I think he does bad things. Anyone who goes out of their way to make themselves look good is usually very bad. And he's there, crouched over a maroon podium, breathing from his chest into the microphone, his forehead gleaming with sweet, his white hair like grains of sand on a cracking earth. What does he do when he gets home? Fucks his wife? What if he fucks his husband. It couldn't be his husband. He's religious.

He could beat his son or daughter. He could rape them too. But we wouldn't ever know that. And his words don't make sense to me. You spout your metaphysical bullshit, so nonspecific I can't form an image in my head because that's what words should do to me, yes? Preachers, shouldn't your words make a beautiful picture in my head and make me go outside and weed the garden of my parents house for free because I usually only do it for money? Do you want me to get on my knees in the dirt for you and pull out your smelly creations? No. You don't give a shit. You lie.

Guy and I are silent.

God, I am scared. That's why I am drinking beer. My trip will go better if I'm drunk. I know I will suffer. I need to suffer. I am so confused. I don't want to suffer. But I need to. I am so scared of the suffering I deserve.

I flip the channel. I can't deal with his throaty bellows and blinking static like we're 20 years ago. A time that is better than this time. At least I think it is. Now is the worst time. Every time is better than this time. My life would be so good if it was another time.

"I wish I slept in today." says Guy.

"How come?" I say.

"I'm tired. You know, last night…"

"Yeah- Sorry about that."

"I had an interview."

"You did?"

"Yeah. And I'm not your fucking babysitter, anyways."

"Why didn't you say something? I didn't even know you had an interview."

"And are you gonna clean up the bathroom?"

"Yeah. I guess. You should have told me."

He is silent again until he stands up and walks to the otherside of the wall and disappears. He'll be fine later.

I walk alone to Luke's along the same path to the bars.

I walk down cement steps below the back porch and grab the knob. It's immobile. Jammed. My knuckle rattles on the door and it hurts. My hand is red and blistered. In my pocket, there is a hairpin. I jam it in.

"Yo!" says Luke as he pulls the door open. I slip the pin in my pocket.

I walk in and flick the knob behind me. They are smoking around the coffee table.

"Your parents are gone?" I say as we walk to the couches.

"Yeah." says Luke.

"Nice. Me too."

"We know."

Everyone laughs.

Through the back door, there is a laundry room. A few desks are laid about on the unfinished flooring with stacks of clothes on top. An old weight set is in the corner of the room and the walls are covered in dense rows of hung up shirts. Through the next door, there is the small coffee table surrounded by an old brown couch. The walls are slated brown wood and strange motivational posters are tacked up everywhere. The TV is on. Michael and Bob and Luke are passing a joint around and they are watching music videos. Their shoulders are relaxed.

I plop down on the couch and set my case of beer down next to me. I crack one and pull out my small tin foil package. Then, I lean forwards and plant my elbows on my knees.

"Here goes nothing, boys." I say while laughing.

"Oh shit. You're trippin?" says Michael.

"Why not?" I say.

"I mean. Don't lose your shit." says Luke. "Can't have that here."

Music is playing in the yellow basement from a small speaker. The air is fresh down here. Outside is boiling and the cicadas trill in the trees. Now, there's only music and conversation. Much later, it will be distorted and the cicadas will sound like the grim reapers scraping scythes, and the walls will be putrid and pouring like pudding. But right now, we are happy. I am happy. My legs tremble a bit. Maybe from the fresh AC, maybe from giddiness. The joint is gone now but I don't want to take my acid just yet.

Luke and I walk outside and find the wooden boards laying against the wall of his garage. A silver keg is resting in a tub of ice. I pump the knob a bit and pour some into a plastic cup I found next to the tub. The beer is foamy and cool. Cooler than the beer in my can. Now warm and flat from the time it was sitting in the sun just outside, as the music plays from the speaker sitting on the table. Led Zeppelin. The Stones. It's Luke's house.

I am standing across from Bob now. I am sucking on a cigarette. It tastes funny. Maybe because I smoked too many last night and there's still a foul taste in my mouth. I forgot to brush my teeth, really. I hope Bob can't smell my breath but we're not even talking. He's looking around the backyard and up to the sky and over to the speaker and he's holding his beer against his side. Then, he takes a step back and shuffles a little and sips his beer and I do the same. I suck on my cigarette with trembling fingers and the beer is warm and gross. There is nothing to do. I get out my tinfoil package and slip out a small baggie from the encasing and put the small tab of paper on my tongue and take a sip of beer as I feel it swell with saliva under my tongue. Like a small bubble it becomes softer and swollen. Now, I have to call Guy.

"Hey. Where are you?" I say.

"Chilling on the couch." says Guy.

"When are you coming?"

"Oh. I don't know."

"I took the acid. You should come."

"God damnit."

"What?"

"I was hoping you wouldn't."

"Just come over."

Luke and Michael have a plastic crate full of bean bags. They toss them by the boards. I'm still sober. Maybe a little drunk. The swollen paper is down my gullet now. I'm not hungry.

Across the yard, there's the big man. Luke's brother. He is smiling. His cargo shorts are long and bits of orange fuzz lining his roundish cheeks. A bent baseball cap sits on his head. He says my name again. I must be looking at him weird.

"Hey, man!" I say. My body is readjusting. It will be normal soon. Until the acid hits.

"Yo!" His arm is still on my shoulder and his other hand carries a case of beer.

Then he walks past me and does the same for everyone. He tells us his friends will be here soon. I don't know them that well. But all of our other friends will be here soon too.

We're inside. Time goes slowly then quickly. Luke has a deck of cards in his hands. My case of beer is huddled beneath my legs, between my feet and the coach. One of my hands is resting against the open cardboard.

Luke distributes the card. I always forget this game.

"Who's coming later?" I say.

"Oh, I don't know." says Luke.

"Yeah. Why don't you relax there, brother." says Michael.

"What? What do you mean?" I say. "I'm relaxed."

My heart is pounding. Their faces are strange. Why are they looking at me? People are so strange.

"I'm just kiddin'!" says Michael. " I just fucking hate those people who you'll text you know, and say come to this party, and they go who's coming over? Am I not good enough for you or something?'"

"What?" I say. "You're good enough for me."

"Am I, though?"

No one is laughing. I force a smile.

"Am I supposed to be here?" I say.

Michael bursts out laughing. I continue to grimace. He puts his arm on my shoulder and tells me he loves me.

I need fresh air. I need a cigarette. Yes. There is a dark hovel somewhere waiting for me. I know which one.

The door closes with a soft thud behind me. I hope it wasn't too loud. Here is my dark hovel. I will calm down before the party here. I am beneath the porch on the damp cement steps, away from the sun and the heat, and I am smoking a cigarette. It makes me feel good. I feel my chest decompressing. The smoke is passing straight through me.

It feels good. Oh my god it feels good. What did I do to deserve to feel this way? Shut up! I don't deserve to feel the beauty of existence. Not like this. This is the bubble I was searching for. Growing. Building up in all of my body and bursting from my eyeballs and painting itself all over my face! Now I can smile! But is it real? I can't believe I'd ever feel this way. So what to do? I burst back into the room and chug a whole beer and they all scream and say hell yeah!

"Dude. Keith Richards is sober now…" says Luke.

"Keith Richards?" says Michael. I can't tell what his face looks like. His eyes are strange. But he looks so happy. Such a happy smile. "Isn't his blood fucking alcohol?"

"Yeah…. They're literally taking away his life source." says Luke.

"Why would they do that to such a beautiful young man." I say.

"He's an old fuck…. He fell out of a tree. That's why." says Michael.

"What?" I say.

"He fell out of a fuckin' tree! In, like, the Bahamas." says Michael.

"What a weirdo." Luke is laughing.

"How much acid do you think that guy has done?" I say.

"Probably enough. I doubt he can actually see things now."

Where is Guy?

"Yeah… He's stuck in a trip. That'd be my guess." Luke laughs. "His thing was heroin, though."

"I wonder what that would be like." I say.

"Probably fuckin' awesome." says Michael. "But really. Don't even think about that."

"But what could it be like?" I say.

"Don't go down that fuckin road. Don't think about it right now."

"Why not?"

"You're on acid. You're gonna wanna do it."

"Why?"

"I don't know. Just don't bring it up."

"Why not?"

"Dude. Shut up about it. You get addicted. Next thing you know, you're homeless."

His face is morphing. I run. I am in the hovel. The darkness. No more strange faces. Just drink.

Now, much later, the sun has set. I am sitting on the bench press talking to some friends.

Jay is standing above me drinking a Miller Lite. His eyes and hands are twitchy but that's okay. He is with a girl. She doesn't know anyone here. She hasn't said a word to anyone. She isn't from here.

"Dude. I love Luke's parties-" says Jay.

"Yeah, man." I say.

I cannot talk or think very well, but I am happy. Not as happy as before, not as happy as I'll ever be. But, I'm happy.

"It's like we're in the 70s-" says Jay.

We look around. Led Zeppelin is still on. Nobody is dressed flashy. Lots of brown shorts and band t-shirts. Someone is in the other room playing the piano and singing. I think it's a Bowie song.

"It's like this basement is a time machine-" I say.

"It might as well be."

I laugh. Then Jay laughs. The girl has an annoyed look on her face and she keeps looking around.

"Wanna have a smoke?" says Jay.

"Thought you'd never ask." I say.

"Jay. I really hate it when you smoke those…" she says.

He shakes his head and swings the door open. Behind the thud fades the Zeppelin and clanging piano keys and the smell of marijuana. The backyard is almost filled and noises are coming from the garage too. I point Jay to the alley way. We walk through the sea of faces.

The gate creaks open. The alley is empty other than garbage cans and trees spilling out over fences and it's all painted in golden light.

We light our cigarettes and the girl stands far back.

"My cousin never showed up." I say.

"How come?"

"No idea."

"That's too bad."

"I'll have to throw another party soon. He's gotta experience this shit. He's been going to sleep way too early."

"Yeah. Nothing like the Southside of Chicago."

"It's so weird. You meet anybody not from here and they look at you like an alien. Like your face is static-y or something."

"I know right… It doesn't help that this place is frozen and the rest of the world is changing so fast."

"Guys… Nobody cares about the Southside…" says the girl.

"Cuz you're not from here." says Jay. He's crossing his arms.

"Anybody who cares about the Southside is someone who can't ever leave. Cuz guess what? Nobody ever leaves."

"How would you know?" says Jay. He's mad.

"Cuz I have eyes." she says.

"You grew up in a cul-de-sac. You don't know what it means. Why are you even weighing in on this?" says Jay. His voice is getting gruff and I'm nervous.

"Cuz you guys are wrong." she says.

"Bout' the world changing?" I say

"Yeah."

"You don't think it's getting worse?"

"Oh. It's getting a hell of a lot worse…." says Jay.

"Okay… It's changing. But it doesn't matter if it's gonna be better or worse. It's gonna change." she says.

"And that's why no one ever leaves the Southside." I say.

"There isn't gonna be anything to leave-" says Jay. "Who the hell do you even become after you leave?

"What are you?" I say.

"I don't know… I'm still from here. I won't ever not be."

"But you left. Did you wanna leave?"

"I don't know."

I think for a minute. Then I understand.

"I know what I want. I want to never be a plumber drinking at Rhino every day. I want to live somewhere else. I don't want to be some engineer or some businessman. I don't want to go to school where everyone tells me shit. Tells me to be fucking normal. See? I'm an independent thinker. I could be the president of the world. But I don't want to be some asshole from the Southside. I don't want to be an engineer. Did I already say that? I don't mean like a tool engineer. I want to engineer ideas. And I want people to like them."

Oh. It's the bubble. It's coming back. I feel so good. I'm so smart right now.

"You know, I think there's a lot of people out there that would like my ideas. I like talking about my ideas." I say.

The cigarette tastes so good.

"There are lots of people out there who have ideas like mine. I don't wanna say I'm not original. But we think the same. Those people out in L.A. I think they do. It sounds like it. Wanna hear my most radical idea?" I say.

Jay is looking at me funny. But it feels so fucking good to talk.

"Leave. Isn't that original?" I laugh. "Destroy it and leave. Fuck it. I don't want to build shit. I want to be a fucking child. I want to be okay. So keep it the same! But it's all so wrong... So we've gotta fix it all. There are good people out there. They're tired of the Southside."

Jay is putting his arm around the girl. She pushes him away. Her face is morphing.

I feel bad for him. I feel so much pity. I'm so sad. I walk to him and try to put my arms around him. His forearms block mine.

"I've gotta go get her." he says.

"I need a hug." I say. "I'm so sorry."

"Dude. I gotta go."

"Please."

I keep trying to wrap my arms around him.

"I gotta go."

Why can't I remember her name? Could be anything. I'm lucky I remember my own name. How am I still coming up? The bubble is back.

"Yo!"

That is a voice I know.

"I've got everything."

Guy is holding a plastic bag. It is my plastic bag. I want to hurt him. It is mine. I am a child.

He is holding a small square. It is tin foil. Yes. I know.

None of this makes sense.

I know.

None of it has ever made sense.

"Guy! Can I have one." I say.

"Another one?" he says.

"Yeah. I'm not really feeling it."

"Well, be patient. That's not a good idea."

I am screaming at him. "I have been. I'm sick of waiting. I don't want to wait anymore."

"All right. All right. Okay. Here you go. Now you have two. I have three so you take care of me tonight. We'll see how you fucking like it."

I wrestle it from his fingers and throw it on my tongue.

I am walking through the backyard with my head down. There is too much noise. Too many people. I feel eyes. Eyes always following me everywhere I go. Even when I am alone. Are those her eyes?

Soon, my eyes do not matter as I rush through the yard. I've been walking for years. The ground has crunched and swirled and the grass grows and dies beneath me. All along this march. I feel the eyes still. The hovel is scary and dark and damp. Oh god. They cannot hear me whimper. No one can. You're not even allowed to!

The door slams behind me. Maybe too hard. There is a group of people on the couch. I can hear them in there talking. I will walk by very quickly and I will talk to no one and I will look at no one. God. They are so scary.

I think. Eyes everywhere. I am. I want.

They watch me climb up the stairs. Clomp. Are they laughing? They probably are. I'm not funny.

I think I slammed the door a little too hard too. I turn the rusting lock and hear the door rattle. I swallow the tab and place my palms on the porcelain sink and breath very slowly. My eyes are shut and I breathe slowly. Okay. It's okay. I breathe. I raise my chin and see the mirror.

The mirror is strange.

There I am. Hunched over. My hair is greasy. It is shiny. My pupils. Black stones in a pond. There is a feeling I cannot understand right now. It is an object with gravity and pull and lines and it is pulling my body and I feel my mind being wiped clean of all the things I have learned. And all the things I have ever learned were incorrect. Fed lie after lie after lie. I know these things now. Just like my face is all a lie and you are a lie. My hands are a lie. See? I will touch myself in the mirror and I will feel something. See as I touch my chest with my palm? I feel a heart beating. But it is not mine. It is just some flesh that tells me it exists so that I survive and fuck someone so that some other kid can be cursed. It is all a lie like my face is reptilian and fuzzy and checkered and it changes every time I blink.

Never have I ever recognized myself. Then a creeping darkness. Then black. Then I am awakened to a trembling thought.

I feel my fingers sliding down my alien body, and like thin snakes, they work at my belt buckle. The metal clangs and my shorts fall to my ankles. My eyes are fixed on them and I wrap my alien fingers around my alien penis. My tears are muffled. My eyes cannot close. My face is shifting from human to human, from male to female, from animal to animal. My thin fingers vibrate. I see the tears falling from the corners of my eyes. At first, they bubble, then seep down my face and onto the cold tile. The faces change at an increasing speed and in accordance, my hand shakes faster. It is all accelerating and a booming rush is blooming inside my ears and it is growing louder and louder and my faces are changing faster and faster and my hand is working and working and working...

A knock! Slight, then booming. Knuckle, then fist.

"You okay in there?" says a voice.

My breath stops. "Yeah." I whimper. "All good."

"People need to get in there, man."

"Okay."

"You need help?"

"No."

"Okay. Hurry up."

What time is it? Where am I? I feel a pop against my sternum as my pupils unglue themselves. And there I am, in my infinite ugliness, the little black and red specks on my face and my face in a strange, strange color. I am gasping. I need air. The room is so small. What time is it? My phone is nothing but a swirl. I can't read. Time to find Guy.

The door creaks and I close it slowly behind me. The corridors stretching to the sides of me are infinite. Until the ends fade into black and the black is racing back towards me. My vision is ending. I slam the door behind me and look down the stairs to the basement. They are wobbly and my legs are too.

But I can do this. I will go downstairs and find my beer and drink this acid away. I cannot remember the last two hours other than brief moments of images that cannot be real. What I have seen is unspeakable. I need to purge them from my memory. All my memory. It all hurts so bad. It can't be true.

The couch is still crowded. I think I can look up. Guy is probably outside. Maybe he is drunk. Maybe he will make me feel better.

The hovel is still damp. But the backyard is beautiful once again. So many people are laughing. And there is Guy. Standing next to the garage all by himself drinking a beer.

"Hey!" I yell.

He looks up to me with a deranged smile.

"Yo!"

I walk quickly to him and grab a beer from the case sitting at his feet.

"How you doin'?" I say. My voice is still shaking.

"Incredible. Where have you been?"

"I don't know."

"Man… You're missing it. I don't know what you're missing but holy shit…"

"I don't know what I'm missing either, but I'm sick of missing it."

"Just let it come to you. That's the only way."

"I thought that's what I was doing."

I am going to get drunk. Guy is wobbly and smiling from ear to ear and laughing infectiously every few seconds. He is okay.

"I need to drink this off." I say.

"No! No. Don't do that. Just let it happen, man."

"It's not working."

"Fucking relax."

"I'm drinking it off."

"Okay… Okay… Okay…"

I don't know how long we've been having this conversation. How long the pauses are between each word. If everything and everyone behind us is flying past.

There he is. His face is alien. But I feel him. I know the beard. I recognize the chin throwing itself back into a laugh. There he is.

He is looking at me. He is standing on the deck with Luke's brother. They are talking and laughing. Why is he here?

He sees me. Oh, no. He is looking directly at me. His eyes are glued to my pupils. I am transfixed. I yank my chin back and drink.

My head comes down. There is nothing left in the warm can. He is walking towards me, with his fuzzy face.

"You were in the bathroom for a while, bud. You doin' okay?" says the cop.

"Yeah. I'm fine." I say.

"You don't look so fine."

"I'm doin' okay."

"You look familiar, bud… What's your name?"

"I don't have one."

The shifting face nods and laughs.

"So you know me?" I ask.

"I think so…" he says.

"Where do you know me from?"

"Ahh… I know." His smile widens. "You were the kid at the bar."

"What are you doing here?" I say.

"I'm here at Tim's party. You?" he says.

"His brother invited me."

"If you had mentioned the other night that you know Tim, it would've been all good."

"I didn't know…"

"Now you do."

"Did you follow me here?"

"What?"

"Nevermind."

"You sure you're doing okay, bud? I'm just here to look out for you. You know… So you don't get in trouble."

"Yes. I'm doing fine."

"You sure you don't need to go home? You're worrying some people."

"Yeah."

"Your pupils are lookin' awfully big…"

I pause. His face becomes his again. His eyebrows are furrowed and his head cocked.

"It's because it's dark."

"Okay."

He crosses his arms.

"Do you know why I had to get you outta that bar the other day?"

"Cuz I'm not 21."

"Nah. That's okay. We're in Beverly… I couldn't just let you talk shit about cops like that. You know why?"

"Why?"

"You see, my dad was a cop. So was my grandpa. You wanna know where they are?"

"Where?"

"Mount Hope. Wanna know why?"

"Why?"

"Sacrifice."

"Okay."

He steps closer and looks me up and down. Really studying me. I'm worried.

"Do you understand now?"

"Yeah."

"Do you really understand, though? I don't think you do…"

After some silence, he laughs. "Thanks, bud. I'll see you around."

And he walks away with a smile.

I have never needed a drink and a cigarette more than right now. I grab Guy's arm who is still laughing and drag him to the alley.

He is stomping around, laughing, speaking nonsense. My head is filled with sentences that do not connect. I have a beer in my hand. I pour it down my gullet and reach for another. I am so angry. That fucking asshole. He fucking followed me here. I know he did. Why the fuck is he out to get me? Another beer. The acid still kicks in. Waves of nausea. A world waving by. Sounds floating by in the wind, unable to be captured by these dumb ears. A world where this alley is golden and forgotten and ignored. Where my cousin will stomp around in a circle, crying, laughing, and screaming follow the leader, as if I am supposed to do anything about this absurd misstep in his life. I am angry and drunk and tripping and I want to yell out. I cannot. They would hear me. Everyone would hear me and I do not want anyone to see me. I know what to do. I crack open another can and pour it down my stomach.

I drag Guy back home. He stumbles and grumbles and mumbles and the way home is confusing. Cars drive past but they pay us no attention. I am grasping a box of beer. They do not care about my booze.

He cries the whole way home. I hold him like a child beneath the moonlight. He cries because he is stuck. He is becoming something other than him. Words have transfixed him, he says. I tell him it is okay. He is stuck in a body that he hates and he cannot ever leave. When he leaves, he'll just inhabit another body, a shell like a cockroach. But he will leave soon and he will transition just as easily. He wants to go there and then he doesn't. While he cries, he can't decide. But his body will give in. Maybe one day, he will not be stuck here.

I put him to bed. He is okay. He is having fun. I can see the smile on his face. He is no longer crying. He laughed about it so he is okay. Now, his lips form a straight line and he sleeps.

I know what to do. I drink more in my kitchen. I crush my nose with my two fingers and gulp down whiskey. I need to drink this acid off. I feel the burn in my throat and a pressure mounting in my stomach. Yes! It's happening. Yes.

I sprint to the toilet and vomit everything. It is yellow and piss colored and tastes like the inside of my stomach. I rush back to the kitchen table and squeeze my nostrils and gulp and gulp until everything hurts.

Now, I know what to do. I stumble as I walk. But I'm just drunk now. I ignore the waviness in the corner of my eyes. I know where to go.

I am on the block. I am closing a wooden gate behind me. Very quietly.

Here is a backyard. A slatted garage in the back. Newly planted fuschias. Pine bushes behind them. A wide window in the back overlooking a kitchen. I am exactly where I am supposed to be.

I creep to the window where a pale light is shining and lift myself just enough to see inside. He is home. He is not stumbling around. He is getting himself water at the kitchen sink. Who else is that? There is a girl lying on the ground. I see the pale light reflecting off her jet black hair.

I watch him drink the water then pick the girl up and move her to the couch. I watch as he begins to caress her black hair with his fingers. Then her cheek. His hand moves down her pale spine and reaches into her pants. I see his fingers digging beneath the denim. I turn to my side and vomit.

What do I do? I am on acid. I am drunk. I vomit again. It makes large splashing sounds. My eyes are watering. I am crying. I reach my chin back up to the window and see him walking towards me. His eyebrows are furrowed. He sees me.

I run away.

Chapter 12 - Is It Heaven?

I know it exists. I've seen it before. Not in my dreams, but something similar. I won't tell you what it looks like. You know what it looks like. You've seen it seep into me, like a quick bubble. And it disappeared as soon as I knew it existed. Then there's just a wall.

You can tell me. I promise. Why are my rational decisions my good ones? No. The choice of life is irrational. The choice to love is irrational. The choice to do anything is irrational. So in the end, an irrational choice always makes more sense. These are the only things that are true. I think.

Now that I can see the truth looking back through a rear-view mirror, I see that my irrational decisions are good. My rational ones are bad. And I have talked to too many rational people to be rational. I despise them. I hate them. They're rational in their choice of life. They walk a straight line. They watch the words coming out of your mouth. You know? Rationality isn't about being objective. It's about being accepted.

So is this why I take it? To see the truth now rather than from the hopeless barrier of history? Is that why? So I can understand myself? Me, me, me, me. The most important being... Is my irrationality what makes me good? Me? I want an answer. Will understanding anything make me good? Will slipping off my mask make me good? I want to be good.

I don't know if it's real, though. I just haven't seen it yet. That's why I need your help. I need you to tell me if it really exists. Even better. Please show me. I beg of you.

Is it relief? Is it death? What am I supposed to understand? I am begging you. The longing feels unfulfillable. But you know. You can tell me. Yes, you can! I'll do anything. You know this... I've told you.

I just did!

Please show me the feeling again. I'll do anything. I want it for real. Don't give me a book. I want it for myself. Don''t you dare give me heroin.

Please. I'll do anything for you.

Chapter 13 - Bad Man

There's the car.

The tree above mine is holding me away from the morning sun. I haven't been awake this early in so long. I am parked along a side street where I can see above the fence and into the wide window.

Something is different. His demeanor is like I've never seen. Last night, I couldn't find him. The same with the last three nights. And the last three mornings. I've been waiting for a knock on my door. I know he's watching me. I haven't gone running in a week. I just tear my muscles hidden alone in my hovel.

There he is, walking across the side street to the parked patrol car. His chest is open, shoulders broad and tall, beard trimmed, and chin raised. He shows no emotion. Now, I want to be like him.

The car starts. I wait a little while before pulling off to follow him. I play no music. I need silence.

He is two cars ahead of me, driving down 103rd street. The patrol car is moving nice and slowly, halting traffic. There is a patient crawl in his movement. I can see through the back window, his chin swinging his head back and forth, checking everything. He is thorough. He probably knows I am following him. I am afraid of that.

On Longwood, he turns left. On 100th, he turns right. I slow down. I don't want him to see me. I am far behind, watching him creep slowly in front of my neighbor's house, just behind the smashed car, then he parks. It's been there for the whole summer. The door opens and he steps out, and looks around the block. He sees my house. He must be thinking. His legs are firmly planted into the cement and all he does is observe. After what feels like an hour, he marches to my neighbor's front door and taps the door with his knuckle. Then his fist. A woman in a bathrobe opens up and they begin to talk. His arm waves around towards the rest of the block. My house. She speaks while leaning forwards, through the door frame, and points about. What the hell are her fingers pointing at? Soon, she steps past the cop and he follows her to the car. They circle it like vultures in silence. Why is he here? She begins pointing up and down the block and I dip down close to the steering wheel and I see them staring at my house. My empty driveway. The mounds of trash bags on the curb. She's telling him where I live.

I turn the car on.

I edge up the block as they stand next to the smashed car. They can't talk any longer. Do I ram his car? No, that's too much.

I pull up next to them and roll my window down. My chest is trembling. Then, I speed down the block staring in my rear view mirror as they continue to talk. Neither recognized me. Maybe he did. He must have. Well, he didn't show it. Maybe he's smart. But he knows my car now. I'm going to have to follow from even further.

Okay. I use the next block to turn around and get the car back in its original position. I watch as he marches back to his car and continues down the block. I follow from far back.

We are travelling down Vincennes now. Dilapidated houses and businesses, forgotten parts of the world, to our right, and a skinny set of train tracks to our left. This is a street you will always see the cops on. It's normal.

At 111th, he turns left. There is a district office further down the road and he parks there. I go further down the street and park on the opposite side. I watch as his stern chest and raised chin move through the door. Now I wait.

I missed him getting back in the squad car. The lights are flashing and the engine makes a loud noise, and he's off. I pick up speed gradually and follow the blinking beacon ahead of me. Where the hell could he be going?

After a mile, he turns left down King Drive. The long boulevard stretches both ways. The patrol car is speeding down the left lane as normal cars pull over along the side. I continue down the left lane, at a safe distance. I see the car pull next to the center of the boulevard, between a set of concrete planters filled with short trees.

I drive past. Two cars missing their front halves sit between the trees. The tarred street is wet with liquid: engine oil, gasoline, coolant, blood. An ambulance is wailing further down the street and I continue forwards and park to the right. I see the scene through my rear view mirrors.

The car is parked on an angle and the blue and red lights blip over and over. The cop has rushed to the car and is violently trying to open the driver's door. I cannot see well through the trees. But there is a body being removed. A face painted in blood, an arm twisted back around and snapped at the elbow. I can see the moans coming from the shattered mouth. I see the cop silent, working. The body disappears along the street. The other officer is hidden, on the other side of the car. He hauls a motionless body with a large gash above its nose and its arms flopping at its side.

From the other car, another motionless body has been removed. It lays on the sunbaked concrete, in the oil and gasoline spills, spilling more blood onto the street. Hands seem to be clutching the stomach, tense in death or seizure.

The cop is waving to the ambulance slowly chugging along, weaving through traffic. The other officer is on his radio now. He is screaming. A firetruck's horn blares from the opposite end of the boulevard. I am so sorry. I did not want to see this. But I cannot stop watching.

Hours pass and I am still in my car. The AC is on low and I have seen them pour sand onto the wet blood and haul them out. I'm getting sweaty. Now the officer wipes his forehead with the back of his forearm, then puts his baseball hat and hops into his car. I wait a block before pulling out.

Further along the road, I see him turn left into the parking lot of an IHOP. They park in front of the windows so I find myself a distant corner spot. Inside, I request a booth far away from him and I watch him. I just want coffee, thank you. Not hungry right now. Maybe in a little bit. Yeah, I'll let you know. Thanks. He eats pancakes and sausages and drinks coffee with an appetite. He shovels it down like he hasn't eaten in weeks. He laughs at things his partner says. He jokes back. He goes to the bathroom. I sit there. And I order pancakes and sausages. I eat them slowly. I cannot finish. I feel sick. I keep drinking coffee and I watch like a hawk. I need to know him like he knows me. I know he's going to try to get me.

They are leaving. I put my head down as they walk through the restaurant. I still cannot tell what the others here think of them. They smell of blood.

Much later, I am following him from a block away. We are driving back towards home. Right on 103rd Street. The streets are filled with people bustling around. I am not sure what they're doing. But everyone is sweating and looking up at the sun like they want to kill it. The officer is back to his chin turning, inspecting every little thing. He won't hesitate to fuck anyone over. That fucking hero.

The car quickly pulls against the curb. I see from far away, two men standing across from each other, chins raised and chests puffed out. Every few seconds, their chests touch and they yell while stepping up onto their toes. Then they back down and yell at each other from a distance. One of the men finally decides to pull his fist back and throws a bunch at the other's face. It is a roundabout hook that misses completely and the other man quickly hits him in the cheek. A crowd is circling around them. One of their cheeks is bleeding now. He steps back and to adjust his pants while the other is holding his fists at his chin. The bleeding man sprints forward and tackles him. The crowd is yelling and huddling around the fight and the sun is baking all of us. The pavement cuts up their skin and blood begins the leak down their spines.

The cop hops out of the car and sprints over, prying at the two men's bodies, but they continue fighting. The cop takes an elbow to the face, and from here, I can see the blood pouring. The crowd begins to yell at the cop, circling around all three.

The partner hops out of the car and I can see his mouth moving but I cannot hear him and the crowd can't hear him either. The partner yanks the cop from the circle and drags him back to the car. They hop back out, with their guns drawn and the crowd disperses. The two fighters are still on the ground, and the cops grab them by their necks and push their faces into the pavement. I leave.

The sun has gone down. There are stars, but barely visible, hidden by all kinds of pollution. I am back under the tree, hidden from the brittle streetlight overhead. I can see the pale glow in the window, but I see no movement.

He appears at the kitchen sink and rubs his hand beneath the cool water. There is defeat in his demeanor now, his shoulders are slouched and he breathes quickly. After running his nose in the water and splashing himself on the face, he walks to the microwave and sticks a plate in. I can see the TV on behind him and I can see his mouth working as he walks to the window. He must have taken a punch to the jaw too. His arms reach for the outstretched blinds and he looks out to the yard and the garage and finally to the street. His eyes stay stuck on the car for a while, then I feel the familiar pull of his pupils. I see his eyebrows furrow. He stands there for a long time staring as my breath picks up. I am frozen.

I jam the keys into the ignition and pull away quickly as my breath sharpens. I'm gasping.

The house is completely dark. I will not allow a light to be turned on in my lonely bunker. I pace up and down my upstairs hallway, waiting. Waiting for what? A phone call? A knock? Where is Guy. I have to call him. He needs to get home. I need him to protect me.

"Hey!" I whisper into the phone.

"What's up?" says Guy.

"Where are you?"

"L.A.. Remember?"

"What? No?"

"What's going on?"

"I think he's coming to get me... He saw me outside of his house and I think he's coming."

"Who?"

"I can't say."

"The devil?"

"No."

"An alien?"

"No."

"You sure there's not a UFO coming to get you?"

Guy is laughing.

"There isn't!"

"Listen, are you on anything?"

"No."

"The devil isn't real, man."

'He's coming!"

"No one is coming. Except for me."

"When?"

"Sooner than later."

"Stop fucking with me!"

"Relax... Relax... No one is coming."

"Okay."

"I can't keep on taking care of you like this."

"What?"

There is a knock at the door.

"He's coming."

Chapter 14 - Special Words

Because I am nobody.

But I've seen you. I see you right now, in the flesh. I see your beauty, I see the knowledge in your eyes. I see how you could kill me at any moment.

That is why I'm so special. I'm the only one who can see you. I'm the only one who knows your secrets. Nobody else gets the special little whispers in their ear.

That is why I'm good. I thought for so long that I was shit. But now, I know I'm good. You're the best thing that's ever happened to me. So tell me what I'm supposed to do. I know you'll tell me the right thing. And I can be good. I can be a fucking hero. I'll be the first hero. And it's all because of you.

So you'll tell me? Right now? I know you chose me. Tell me you did.

Okay... Honestly. I want to say I am sorry. I think you're really the best. I am thankful for all the help and advice. I hear you. I really do. It has to be this way. I want to be a hero. That is above all metaphysics. I want to be good. I want to transform. I am so sorry for what happened. You've heard everything. I want to be a hero. Just like you.

We're the same. Me and you. Both victims of the world and victims of life and victims of experience. So I understand why there is no other choice. I get it. I understand. Finally. For once, I understand. And it's not just in a lonely moment, it's forever.

Chapter 15 - Meeting You

I smell the air now that I am awake. The light is thin. Clouds overcast and I scurry about pretending I have strength. This morning is all a fucking joke. I woke up to the guttural screams of a beautiful woman next door to me. There is only one word she spoke. It was one I knew. But then both of them emerged and we all laughed about it downstairs, in the bare kitchen, without a trace of all the garbage from earlier. It's Saturday. It's Guy's birthday. His friends are here and we sit around the kitchen table drinking coffee and scrounging for whatever food we can get our hands on. I walk to the patio and smoke a cigarette. We are down to the last of our acid and I'm ready to finish it tonight. Guy and I are gonna take it all. He promised we would.

There are six of us at the table. Three are going to leave soon. And later than that, we will be taking our acid. Then they will come back and we will have a big party. I am excited for tonight since summer is winding down and school will start again and I will find myself clenching a blanket throughout the night that will become weeks and straining my teeth and eyes as I try to find sleep in a dark infinite cavern.

Guy's friend is cool. His hair is short and curly and he smiles and laughs a lot. The rest are gone for now. I think he'd be a good friend to have around all the time. But he's not from Chicago. Better on him.

"Anyone wanna play basketball?" says Guy.

"Sure." I say.

"Yeah." says Guy's friend. His name is Matt.

They walk to the patio and I grab a basketball from the basement. Just a plastic one left sitting around. It's okay. It's gonna get dirty on the wet court anyways.

I keep sliding and Guy keeps bumping me with his elbow. Matt doesn't want to sprint. He's being careful and shooting from far away. Every time he does, Guy digs his elbow into my rib. I elbow him back. I hear him breathing hard. He gets the ball and dribbles it to the back. Matt isn't good at defense. So when Guy gets past him and comes sprinting in for a layup, I push him and he misses the shot.

"What the hell are you doing?" he says.

"No easy shots." I say.

"Yeah. Okay."

His ball up top. I'm guarding him now. His eyes are burning into mine. I don't know what I want to do. I don't want him to keep hurting me. I have to defend myself. So when he blows past me, I grab his arm as he shoots. The ball clangs off and he goes sprinting after it. When he puts on the breaks, his right leg continues forward and we hear a small pop. His face turns into a grimace and he starts to yell as he falls to the ground.

There's a part of me that's happy. Better him than me. That's what you get.

Guy is groaning and twisting on the ground. His jaw is clenched and eyebrows tight. I feel sorry for him. This is not good. Matt and I carry him up the stairs and through the kitchen and lay him down on the couch. He leans back and brings his leg up sideways onto the couch.

"It really fucking hurts. God fucking damnit" he says.

I go get him some ice.

Later, he is still laying on the couch. He's very sad and he keeps looking at me strangely. I don't think it was my fault, but his jaw has been clenched all morning. He doesn't want to take the acid anymore. He thinks he really did something. He doesn't want to have the party anymore. There's something wrong with his knee. But it's okay, I'll convince him. So I hand him a beer and he takes it. Maybe I'll get him drunk so the pain goes away and we can all have fun together.

In the kitchen, I move the side table against the wall. I collect all the paintings from the wall in the kitchen. My great aunt's drawing. Her eyes still follow me in the kitchen. In the dining room, I collect small dishes and fragile vases and add them to the pile. It is all a fragile pile. I bring them up to my parents room and arrange them on the bed. I put a few of the paintings and the drawing behind the headboard just in case. In the backyard, I set up a table on the patio and clear off the kitchen table. I think this is enough. It's gonna be the biggest party yet. My beer is in the fridge. I find the baggie of mushrooms and acid. I think Matt is taking mushrooms. He came with a carton of milk. That's in the fridge too. My lightshow is set up too. It's going to be the most beautiful trip of my life. Before everything goes to shit again.

I like to think about the outdoors in these moments, when I am preparing for an acid trip. It's something everyone says. But I think they are right. It doesn't matter how far away we get from it, it's always gonna call us back. It's not something to hide from or ignore. It's the most beautiful thing in the world. Our limitations and flaws. That's what I'm gonna think of tonight.

We are sitting together in the living room. Guy is laying on the couch. Matt and I on either side. I told them I was taking mushrooms for Guy on his birthday, it feels right. Matt was taking some mushrooms too. Not too many. Just enough to get him loose.

"Okay. Guy, we're still gonna have the party tonight even though you're not tripping, Guy. You okay with just drinking?" I say.

"We shouldn't," he says.

"Why not?"

'I'm not in the mood."

"Just get drunk, you'll be okay."

"We shouldn't have the party. How many more are we gonna have? I'm sick of it."

"I invited a bunch of people already, I can't just cancel."

"Why not?"

"Because I don't want them to be mad at me. And it's your birthday."

"I'm asking to not have the party."

"It's too late. You're gonna have fun. And what about Matt and your other friends?"

He says nothing as he scowls. Then, he brings the beer up to his mouth.

It's later now. The party is starting soon. We haven't moved from our spots. I shove two grams into my mouth and wash them down with a beer. In all my time alive, I haven't tasted anything worse. Matt takes a gram. He's just hanging out. My friends are gonna be here soon.

We are all at the kitchen table. Not many people are here yet. Guy walks with a limp and talks with a scowl. Matt is chugging milk and then beer. He'll be fine. I think the mushrooms are scaring him.

"Yo. Is it cool if my buddy Joe comes?" says Luke.

"If you finish your beer." I say.

"And my brother?"

"Make it two."

"You gotta fuckin' do it!" says Michael from across the room.

They crowd around him and yell until two beers are in his stomach. He burps and holds his stomach and slowly stands up. Soon, he is puking over the side of the railing. Everyone is laughing. The music is loud and I am happy. But I'm not really tripping. I'm drinking my beer slowly. I should be tripping by now. I find the baggie and stick two more grams in my mouth and chew with a grimace and wash them down with beer. There. I should be fine now.

I am walking through the living room now. There are five people I have never met on the couch and their beer has spilled. A table is in there now. I have never seen that table before and there is a crowd around it. The music is too loud. I hear yells and shouts from everywhere. In the kitchen, the island is sinking underneath the spilled beer and the floor squeaks and there are traces of mud and the whole place smells of sweat. Where are my friends? I don't see anyone I know. I am not tripping yet. I am drunk. Where is everyone? I shouldn't have done this. It's too much. The back porch is filled too and I hear voices up on the back roof. I am on the patio. Smoking a cigarette. I need a break. I need to be alone. There is too much. Blue and red lights flash out front and I hide. Someone will take care of it. I will smoke my cigarette and pretend it is not happening. People will be quiet.

Much later, I am still not tripping. I am down by the light show but nothing is happening. I am so frustrated. I let myself space out and allow the colors and music and lasers to take me far from here but nothing happens. Two more grams. 30 more minutes. Nothing. There's too much sound up there. I go upstairs. I go to the back porch to smoke a cigarette. The house has cleared out and people are filling up the patio now, yelling. My friend has a rig sitting on the table out here. I watch him heat up some wax and he coughs out smoke. A huge cloud. The backyard smells fresh in the thick wind. He looks to me.

"Take a hit."

"I took shrooms."

"I thought you weren't feeling it."

"Nah. I'm not."

"Take one. It'll help."

"You sure?"

"Yeah."

I hunch over the table and press my mouth to the pipe. I hear the blow torch next to my ear and he asks if I'm ready. I nod. The smoke is harsh and it hurts my chest. I keep breathing in as hard as I can and it's so painful but I keep going and I hold it until it all bursts out into the night sky. I cough and cough until I'm breathless. I thank him. I'll go to my light show now.

I'll wait 15 minutes. If nothing happens, I'll go drink until I blackout and hopefully my body does the rest. The lights pass on by and I feel nothing. The purple reminds me of an ancient emotion, one I might not feel ever again. Blue is just blue. I am not a human right now. I expect to understand something when I feel this numb, but a fog overtakes my brain. To reduce everything to simple truths. My thoughts are hidden by walls of mist. They swirl around like kaleidoscopes. I am numb and I am empty. The colors mean nothing to me. Reduced truths mean nothing to me.

I see a shimmering language glistening on the wall. It is curved and it is ancient, encrusted on patterns I have never seen before. The shapes look as if they have been pressed into the yellowing sandstone wall by an ancient tribe, thousands of years ago. The language floats off the wall now and dances like a flag in the wind. It is a shining language I cannot read. One so foreign only my subconscious can only react. I want to read it. I want to understand. And I strain my eyes. Then time stops. The light is frozen on green. The patterns and language have evaporated. The music is dead silence. The lasers aren't there anymore. I just see the green light on the white wall and nothing else. I cannot move my head because I am surrounded by the darkness of space. There is nothing around me but silence and blackness. I am not being flushed. I have just ceased existing. And a feeling is building in my heart. A feeling that hurts so bad and I am so scared. I have never been so scared in my life. It is bursting from me like a little bubble. I scream. Without noise. I try to shake my head. There I am. There is the basement. I am me again. I am no longer face to face with a fucking green wall. I am alone in this fucking basement. This fucking hovel.

I sprint all the way upstairs. I pace. I pace. Up and down the hallway. My chest is pounding. I can't stop moving. The hallway is wiggling all around me. I feel so sick. I am so scared. I call for Guy. My voice is barely loud. It's a squeak in an empty universe. It trembles from my mouth. It drips out like a rusty faucet. I let the fear take over. I call out his name again.

Two feet for each step. I hear the squeak every time. I cannot stop pacing. My hands are shaking. I hear the squeak with every step. It's been two years since I heard the first one. Why will time not go? Why will it not accelerate until the bitter end?

There he is. I hear his voice. It's following me. He's downstairs. I know. He's following me. He's still here. He's right behind me.

There he is. There's Guy. He is limping through the hallway, the light shining behind his head walking towards me, darkness.

"I am so scared." I whimper.

"What's going on." says Guy in a dark tone as he continues towards me. I cannot see his face but his shoulders are wide like shadows.

"I don't know. I'm just so scared." I say while pacing slowly.

"This is why I told you not to have a fucking party."

"It's not them."

"What is it then?"

"I don't know... I just wanna leave here. I don't wanna be here. There's nothing here. There's just fucking noise."

"What? And come to L.A. with me? You think that's gonna happen?"

"No."

"Then what? What the fuck do you want?"

"I don't know."

"That's your problem. You don't fucking know anything."

"What do you know?"

"I know how not to be an asshole. You know, since I moved here, my life has gone downhill. Not in the sense that I lost my job or my fucking girlfriend broke up with. It's living with you. You're a fucking burden. You're a parasite."

"Fuck you!"

"I wasn't gonna say it. I was gonna wait. Call it a fucking day. But this is too much. You fucking suck."

"Shut the fuck up."

"No. You need to know it."

Okay. He's bad.

"Who the fuck are you? Going to L.A.? I've been thinking about it… How you think L.A. is so great. The pinnacle of humanity. Or whatever the fuck you say. And I realized, it's no different from any fucking place."

"Fuck off. You don't know anything."

"I know that nothing changes in L.A. It's the same shit. Just like here. And people go there to jerk themselves off. Like you're doing."

"What? Cause I want a happy life? Money?"

"No. Because you're lying."

"I'm lying? Listen to yourself. You're fucking lost."

I am on the verge of tears as the hallway spins around me.

"Guy. I'm sorry. Help me."

"I'm not taking care of you. I'm done with this shit."

"Fuck you."

"No. Fuck you."

"Yell at me some more."

"What?"

"It feels good when you yell at me. Does it feel good when I yell at you?"

"What? No?"

"Come on. Please. I want you to. I want to understand. That's what it feels like when you yell at me."

He shakes his head in disgust one more time.

"Go to fucking bed."

I listen to him limp down the steps. My eyes are wet. I sprint holding them shut until I have my light show and I bring it back upstairs. Yes. To my hovel. I'm tripping too hard.

The show is on my ceiling. I want to be good. I'm sorry, Guy. But I am still so empty. I want to understand the small truths they talk about. There is new music in my ears. The party downstairs is normal. Yes, that is the truth. I am not afraid. I keep telling myself that. The music is good. It is the best.

The lights are changing and I can feel them again. I want the secret language to show itself but for now I only see the same colors. The blue and purple are good. They make me feel human again when I wasn't for so long. I can feel them now, breathing my rationality and irrationality back into place. Now, I can see what is good. And that I am not good. I am horrible. And I am stuck. And I can let myself hide in the purple beauty I see up on the ceiling and the changing notes bouncing around my scared brain. And I will be okay. Maybe I can be like this forever. Maybe I do not need to change. Maybe, this is it. Now, I am okay with it. I have seen the darkness within me. It is something I will not speak of. I know now. I understand that this is it. A color wheel on a wall and I assign beauty to those colors and I bask in masturbatory happiness and waste away. That is okay.

That is when I see you. A face is materializing in the blue. Then it disappears when the purple comes. Fucking stop it purple. Stop it red. Stop coming. Please. I scramble for the lightshow with trembling hands. I am trying to find the setting.

Stupid buttons. Yes. The only blue setting. Yes. There you are. I stand up on my bed.

It is the woman. She still stares at me even up here. Now she is blue. Her eyes, gaping holes. Her hair long and thin and blue-black and her teeth are perfect and angry. She does not blink. I see her body now. Thin like a peasant. White like a whale. She stands against my wall and stares at me with those gaping eyes. They suck me in. I am so afraid. I fall to my knees before you.

I will tell you everything.

Chapter 16 - It Happens

Would you stop staring at me?

No! I can't stop. I can't stop pulling my hair out. The pain feels too good. You told me to in the first place. I need to stop. I need to stop hurting myself. I will go get your picture. We'll all be together.

The hallway is wavy. My hand holds me against the wall as I march to my parents room and I tremble. There is so much noise downstairs but I do not care. Here I am, I understand.

The paintings and dishes and vases have all been moved. A turquoise vase is laying on the floor. Where are you? Behind the headboard. I pull the bed out a little. There you are. You're just laying on the floor. I hear your little voice whispering. Something stings my finger. There's blood on the tip. Your frame is cracked and the glass is broken. I collect the shards. I am so sorry. I have you now.

You are still on the ceiling and you are in my hands. Your perfect picture. I know what to do now. You told me.

I swim through the swarm of flesh and find him. I grab his collar. Where is he? No one can hear me over the music. All I see is a shrug. No one looks. No one cares. I find Michael. I yell at him. I beg him. Where is he? Where is that motherfucker? He shakes me off and laughs. His eyes grow concerned and he walks away. He doesn't understand why you're here with me. Nobody understands.

Luke. He must know. Where is he? I am pushing my way through body after body, like I am swimming upstream. There he is. Sitting up on the countertop, laughing. Where is he? I yell. Why isn't he here with your brother? He shakes his head. He pushes me away. I know where he is. I know.

Guy is sitting alone on the front porch, drinking a beer. He sees me walk out with my strange instruments. He ignores me. So I walk alone.

The pale light is on. The fuschias tremble in the back of the garden. The gray garage is hidden in the gray light. I try the handle but it jams. I can't make any noise. I can do this. And I can pick a lock. Even in my fucked up, genius state. Yes, I am a genius. I am God. You hear me? I can save you. I can do it. I came ready. Now I'm inside. We're here. You know this place? God. I am so sorry. You know it.

Which one is his room? I can find it. I have to be quiet. I can't turn on any other lights. It's completely silent. It's just me, you and him. The walls aren't wavy here. Is it there? No. That's a laundry room. That looks like a bedroom. Yes it is. That's a lump. I am going to put you down now. Okay?

You rest on your back on the carpet.

I walk to the lump. It's a black mound on a white bed. I pull the shard of glass from my back pocket. I squeeze. I don't care how much it hurts and how much I will bleed. I plunge down at the stomach. I feel it shudder under the rough glass. But it goes in still and tears skin as it comes out. I hear a gentle moan. And I plunge down again. The mound is moving and shaking. I plunge down again. The mound can't move much. Suddenly and behind me, the light clicks on.

There he is, one final time. There is a trickle of blood coming from the corner of his mouth and I can see the inside of his stomach. His chest is heaving slightly as the pool of blood forms around him. God, I have never felt this way before. I see the intestines. They look like gummy worms, wriggling around in a hollow cavern. God, I feel so happy. I have never felt such relief. But my right hand is covered in blood.

I hear a soft breath behind me. I turn around. An old woman is standing there, blanketed in a white nightgown, in the doorway. She stares at the blood leaking from my hand and the shard and she sees him in the bloody bed, breathing his last breaths. Her mouth opens and gapes like a fish but no sound comes out.

I begin to mutter. She has seen everything. She knows my eyes. I whisper as I walk to her. I tell her I'm sorry. A ball is growing in my throat. I never wanted to do this. But I have to. I'm so sorry. I'm so sorry.

And I walk to her but she doesn't move. She doesn't make a sound. She stares back up at me and her eyes tremble. I begin to sob as I jab the shard over and over and over into her stomach and I feel her slouch forward, her shoulders pushing against my stomach. I hear small gasps and exhales and I hear soft cries. I feel pity. And I sob and I sob as my arm works like a machine. Her forehead comes to rest against my chest as her knees give out.

I shove her away to the white carpet and blood pools around her frail skin and bones. The color is dragged from her face already. The cop behind me continues to gurgle as I crash to the floor. And for a long time, I sit against the bed and watch the old woman leak and listen to the cop's gurgles and my tears do not stop.

Here, in the alley, it is perfect nighttime. The soft glow from the streetlights pour over me. When I close my eyes, I can no longer see you. I own the world, now.

Much later, I am in my bedroom. It's all too much. The sirens bounce around my head. My hand still bleeds, wrapped around the shard of glass. I raise it to my neck and gulp. I pull the tip through the thick vein on the right side. It hurts. I see black. But I've been there before. I've seen the wall, strangled by creeping Charlie.

55189319R10079